HER DIRTY MOUNTAIN MEN

A REVERSE HAREM ROMANCE

MIKA LANE

HEADLANDS PUBLISHING

BE THE FIRST TO KNOW...

Want more heat, heart,
and bad boys who know what they're doing?
Join my list and I'll send the steam straight to your inbox,
starting with a deliciously naughty story:

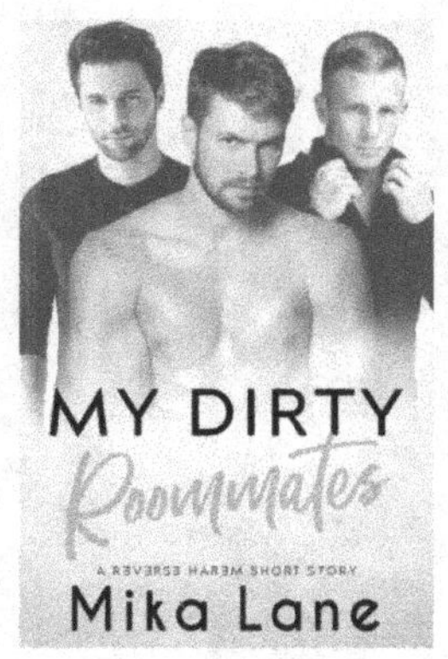

SIGN UP TO MY MAILING LIST!
Or visit:
https://geni.us/free-book-signup

AVA STONE

IT WASN'T THAT I DIDN'T LIKE THE MOUNTAINS. I JUST
didn't *do* mountains.

They were pretty and all, but also dirty, and spider-y,
and worst of all, a long way from the city.

But there I was, heading up Deep Water Mountain, the
highest peak in the state, in my struggling little VW Bug. I
knew I should have bought the turbo model.

I also should have filled up on gas before I'd left the
main road.

But it was all good. I hadn't been to the mountain to
visit my Uncle Bo since I was a kid, but I did recall it
wasn't all that isolated. There were gas stations and stores
all over.

Right?

But proof that my memory might not be what I thought it was, the 'low fuel' warning on my dash had been screaming for fifteen minutes. Initially, I'd been sure a gas station would be right around the corner, but as I moved through the mountain's switch-back roads and rounded one empty corner after another, I got nervous.

Real nervous.

And to make matters worse, I'd poorly estimated how fast my car would go through the remaining gas it had. Climbing the mountains in it sucked up gas faster than in the city, where the roads were pretty much flat.

My lousy calculations hadn't taken that into account.

And now I had a problem.

The Bug, which had been sputtering for the last minute or so, gasped one last time, lost power, and finally died. I had enough momentum to pull over onto a skimpy gravel shoulder, but on the narrow mountain road, there wasn't much room. I was right in the way of traffic. If there were any traffic, that was.

Well, shit.

I looked ahead, then behind me, and all I could see was an endless tunnel of trees that disappeared into the far reaches of my view.

Great. Just great.

I'd run out of fucking gas in the middle of fucking nowhere.

Because I was a fucking idiot.

And my cell phone had no signal because that's exactly how my day was going. Another reason to dislike the mountains—unreliable cell service. It was the freaking twenty-first century. Why couldn't cell phones work everywhere?

I pounded on the horn, not because anyone would hear me but because it felt good to have a grown-up temper tantrum. There were only so many options when you were stuck inside a car.

I could see the news story now.

Woman found dead in her VW Bug on a remote road on Deep Water Mountain.

A young life cut short by poor planning.

I hadn't been to the mountain since I was a kid of maybe ten or so. I couldn't be sure. But I did remember being enchanted by Uncle Bo, his cabin, and the woods that surrounded it.

Of course, that was back before I had issues with any place not within a ten-mile radius of civilization.

And now Uncle Bo's place was mine. Not sure yet whether that was a good thing or bad.

The rumble of a truck pulling up startled the shit out of me. The driver pulled over, and in my rear-view mirror, I watched him approach my car in a rugged *I chop wood* sort of way.

I double-checked that my doors were locked and grabbed the pepper spray out of my purse just as he rapped his knuckles on the passenger side window.

"You okay?" he asked, his voice muffled through the closed window.

Holy crap. When did they start making mountain men so hot? Not that I'd ever known any for comparison. But still.

I opened the passenger window about two inches.

"Hello. I'm fine. Thank you for asking."

I returned to my phone, scrolling intently, as if I were about to make contact with another human who would be able to get me out of my shitty situation.

Yeah, right.

But in spite of my dismissiveness, he stayed there, looking in my window.

I sneaked a glance and saw him rubbing his face and frowning. He looked up and down the road.

And that's when I realized I was probably about to die.

I tucked the pepper spray up my sleeve with shaking hands. It would be only a matter of seconds before he busted through my window with a giant axe or some such, unlocked the door, and dragged me off to wherever crazies living in the mountains took their victims.

Oh, why hadn't I just stayed home? I didn't need to see the little cabin Uncle Bo had left me in his will. It wasn't like I was going to live there, or even visit aside from this one trip to check it out and meet with a real estate agent. I could have handled everything over the phone without a single trip to the mountains.

But no. I had to see it for myself. Figure out how much money I'd pocket after its sale.

Because I had *plans*. I knew the sale of the cabin would not be a windfall of staggering amounts of cash, but it had to be some sort of tidy sum—enough to help me buy a nice condo in an apartment complex with a pool and pretty landscaping.

Was that too much to ask? To get out of my crummy little rental?

But before I could even get started, here I was, the perfect subject for one of those crime shows my mother watched every night.

What a way to be remembered. My mother would watch a melodramatic TV 'documentary' about how her only daughter had met her untimely end. It was one thing to die in my car of starvation and dehydration, but another altogether to be taken by a murderous maniac.

My presumed abductor knocked at the window again, this time leaning down enough that I could see his entire face.

His handsome ruggedness was scary and brutish, accented by a shaved head, heavy brow, and facial scruff.

"Well, okay," he said through the small window opening. "If you're sure you're all right, I'll be on my way. But be careful. The shoulder here is narrow and you're half parked in the road. Not a lot of cars come by these parts and I'd hate for someone to plow right into you."

I looked back at my phone. My mother always said not to stare at scary people. "Okay. Thanks. See ya." I waved.

In my mirror, I watched him return to his truck, his gait heavy and confident. He must have been over six feet tall and with his plaid flannel shirt blowing in the wind, a nicely muscular ass appeared to be underneath his blue jeans.

Gross. Was I crushing on a mad man?

He got behind the wheel, looked at his watch, and pulled back out onto the road.

"Wait!" I screamed, jumping out of the VW and right into his path.

His brakes squealed and even though the truck windows were closed, I heard him swear.

"Jesus fucking Christ!"

I ran to his window, which he slowly opened.

Who was the crazy now?

"Hi, I'm so sorry. But I do need help. I'm out of gas," I blurted, wringing my hands.

He scowled and rolled his window down the rest of the way. "Miss, I almost ran you down with my truck."

I stood on my toes, the truck was so high. "Yeah, that was stupid. I'm sorry."

His knuckles were white from gripping the steering wheel, and he looked straight ahead, avoiding my pleading gaze.

Of course, I could make him understand. "I just... I just am not familiar with this area, and was afraid. You know. Of *you*."

His eyebrows rose and he looked back at me. "Okay. You're out of gas?"

I fluffed my hair and gave him my best smile. "Yeah, can you believe it?" I giggled.

He looked at me like he could easily believe it. And that he thought I was a nutcase. Couldn't really blame him.

First, he offered help and I sent him packing.

Then, I changed my mind and jumped in front of his moving truck.

And last, I'd admitted to running out of gas in the middle of freaking nowhere.

He sighed and nodded. "All right. Let me pull over."

I stepped out of the way while he maneuvered the truck back to the side of the road.

This time when he got out, he kept a safe distance, probably assessing my mental state. "How'd you run out of gas, anyway? This place is pretty desolate. You didn't see the signs saying 'no more gas for fifty miles?'" He'd used finger quotes to emphasize his point, in case I had missed it.

Which I hadn't.

And what signs was he talking about anyway? I didn't see any freaking signs.

"I must have missed them," I said sheepishly. "I thought for sure there'd be a gas station around the corner, but I kept driving and driving and never came across one."

"That's because there aren't any." He reached into the cab of his truck and pulled out a gas can.

Ohthankgod.

"There used to be."

His head whipped in my direction. "I thought you said you weren't familiar with the area."

Shit. I *did* say that.

"I visited here when I was a kid. Long time ago. And I could swear there were gas stations."

He opened his mouth to say something, closed it, and headed to my gas tank, shaking his head.

No need to tell him my whole story. He was kind

enough to help, but when it came down to it, I still didn't know him from a hole in the wall.

Even if he were freaking gorgeous and saved me with his can of gas.

"How long you up here for?"

Damn. I knew there would be questions.

"Oh, just a quick trip," I said breezily.

He screwed the gas cap back in. "Where you staying? You got a house up here?"

Shit, shit, shit.

"Oh, over at the motel."

He frowned. "*What* motel?"

"Um. The new one." I pointed in some random direction. Like that would throw him off.

"There's no new motel."

I nodded. "Yes. There is. It might be so new you don't know about it."

He shook his head at me. "Um, okay. I gave you a couple gallons. Plenty to get to a gas station safely. Now can you start your car, please?"

I jumped behind the wheel and my baby started right up. Thank god.

He looked satisfied. "All right. You're good to go. But do me a favor. Don't come up here again with less than a quarter tank of gas."

Seriously. The next person who stopped to help might not be as nice.

Or as good looking.

I nodded. "You're right. Great advice."

He stood there like he wanted to chat.

"Oh my god. Where are my manners?" I reached in my purse and pulled out a twenty, which I thrust at him. "Will this cover it?"

He waved his hand at me. "You don't have to pay me. Please be more careful next time."

He continued standing there. Was I missing something?

I thrust the money at him again. "Then take this as a tip. I mean, you work for a gas station, right? Isn't that why you have gas?"

The corner of his mouth turned up, but I wouldn't call it a smile. "No. I do not work at a gas station. And thank you for the offer, but I'm good."

Turning, he headed for his car, and without looking back, he hit the road.

2

AVA STONE

Only one week prior, some man had called me and introduced himself as Uncle Bo's attorney. Which was strange in itself, because Uncle Bo was not the kind of guy to have attorneys or any of the things other, more conventional people did.

He just wasn't that sort of guy.

Which I'd loved as a kid. My mother, who was his much-younger sister, not so much.

We'd visited him a couple times when I was a kid, my parents and I crammed into his one extra bedroom. It was tight and cozy, but I loved it, in part because Bo was so cool. I didn't remember much more than that except that the trips had come to an abrupt stop.

From what I'd gathered by eavesdropping on my

parents' conversations, my mom was frustrated he'd never done anything with his life, and that he might not be the best influence on me.

I didn't understand how such a cool guy could be a bad influence on anyone.

After that, there was no more seeing Uncle Bo. The occasional letters from him dwindled to postcards, which became yearly holiday cards, and after a couple years, those petered out too. Bo faded from my mind the way out-of-sight people do for kids, and the only time I thought of him was on the rare occasion my parents talked about him.

In a perfunctory way, the attorney told me Uncle Bo had died.

Why was he calling to tell me and not my mother?

So it was completely out of the blue when he went on to say I'd inherited Bo's cabin on Deep Water Mountain.

That about knocked me off my chair.

Me?

Uncle Bo had left me his cabin? I'd not seen him in almost twenty years. But I did remember liking the cabin. Even loving it.

But I could barely picture it—or even Bo—anymore.

And what was I going to do with a cabin in the mountains, anyway?

When the attorney handed over the key to the place, he also gave me the name of a local real estate agent. And a contractor. He hadn't seen the place in years, he told me, but said it probably needed work.

"You may want to sell," he'd said. "I don't think it's worth much, but I don't see you keeping it."

That seemed to be the prevailing sentiment.

"Oh, sell it, honey," my mother had said.

"Sell. Definitely sell," my best friend Suki had said.

"Ugh. Get rid of it," my boss had said with a wave of her hand.

So now I was heading up to the cabin to see what needed to be done before I could put it on the market.

Needless to say, I felt shitty for not being a better niece. I could have kept in touch with my uncle, even against my mother's wishes. But that hadn't occurred to me. Not once. You don't think of things like that when you're a kid. And once I was an adult, I didn't think of him at all.

Before I'd hit the road, I'd called both the real estate agent and contractor. The realtor was all too happy to come over, hoping to make some money with minimal effort. The contractor was another story. I should have listened to him.

"Um, Miss Stone, have you been to this… um, cabin?"

"Oh yeah. I used to go there as a kid. I haven't been there in almost twenty years, but I remember it was awesome. Totally old school with logs for walls and stuff—"

"Okay, Miss Stone. Give me a call once you… see it again, and we'll set up a time to meet. If you still want to."

It was a warning that went right over my head.

Running out of gas had set me back a good hour on my estimated arrival, but there was a sliver of daylight left as I pulled down the narrow lane leading to the cabin.

My VW bounced violently over the rutted dirt road. I actually considered leaving it and walking the rest of the way to avoid damage, but I couldn't remember how much further the cabin was and didn't want to lug my belongings.

Fortunately, this trip was a one-time thing because a car like mine was not meant for off-roading. If I had trouble with it, who would help? I might not always be as lucky as I was today.

Crap. I should have gotten the gas guy's phone number.

Hey before you leave, can I get your number in case I have more car trouble?

He would have loved that.

Finally, I neared the cabin. The light was getting low so I couldn't see much until I was on top of it, but when I saw the structure, I turned my headlights on.

Big mistake.

3

LOGAN MEYER

"LOGAN, WHAT TOOK YOU SO LONG? IT'S TOO LATE NOW TO work on the bridge."

Theo looked up at the waning sun while he pulled on his thick suede work gloves and started helping me move lumber out of the back of my pickup truck.

"I know, man. I'm sorry. It took me longer than I thought to get supplies, and then I stopped to help a damsel in distress."

Theo's jaw dropped. "What? You ran into a *woman* in these parts?"

We put the lumber on a large wheelbarrow we'd devised for moving bulky things around our property, and maneuvered down a narrow path to the creek on the boundary of our land.

Theo was moving too fast to be safe. If he dropped one of those boards on my foot, I was going to be fucking pissed.

"Listen to this. The woman was in a VW Bug, sitting there pulled over, half on the shoulder, half on the road. I was like *what the fuck?* I pulled over and must have scared the shit out of her because at first she blew me off, saying she was fine and thanks anyway. She wouldn't even look at me. I figured, okay, suit yourself."

Theo turned around. "You were just going to leave her?"

"What else was I going to do? She wouldn't take any help. Anyway, as I was pulling back into the road, she jumped in front of the truck, screaming and asking for help. I almost ran her over. She was like a crazy woman. First, she acted like *I* was an axe murderer, then, she wouldn't let me go."

Theo laughed. "Guess it's your ugly mug that scared her, buddy. They take one look at you and run screaming."

I flipped him off for fun. "I wouldn't talk if I were you. It's not like they're lining up to get a whiff of your hippie ass long hair and smelly armpits."

Theo raised his arms in the air. "I take great pride in my smelly armpits."

"I'm glad somebody does."

We reached the creek and stopped to catch our breath before unloading the lumber.

"So anyway, she said she was visiting, but she wouldn't say where she was staying. She was totally evasive. In fact, she said she was staying at the 'new motel,'" I said, using air quotes.

Theo's jaw dropped. "New motel? What new motel?"

Exactly.

"It was clear she was bullshitting me, but she didn't back down. Whatever. I don't give a damn where she was going. I gave her a couple gallons of gas and sent her on her way. But hey, she tried to tip me. She thought I was a gas station attendant."

"Dude, you should have taken her money just to fuck with her and asked if you could be of further service. Maybe you could have cleaned her windows." Theo laughed, slapping his thigh.

Funny guy.

"No thanks, man. She was one of those high maintenance types. Tight jeans, high-heeled boots, fake fur jacket. What she's doing up here on the mountain is beyond me."

High maintenance but *beautiful*. Although I kept that fact to myself. I didn't need any more ribbing.

We returned to the truck for our next load. It was a pain in the ass to move building materials around our heavily wooded property, but there was no alternative. I wasn't really complaining, though. I liked being active. As a builder, I'd always been a physical person before moving to the mountain, and was even more so now.

"What'd she look like?"

I knew he'd go there.

"You know, she was pretty in a big city way with her

painted nails and long, smooth hair. Hadn't seen a woman like that in a long time."

Shit, not since before I'd left my father's business building homes.

"I hope you were nice to her because she's probably the only hot woman you're gonna see for a long time."

He was right. We saw more elusive mountain lions these days than pretty women.

"COLTON'S NIGHT TO make dinner. I'm psyched, man," I said, pulling a beer out of the fridge.

It was almost always Colton's night to make dinner. He was the best cook of the three of us, and besides, loved doing it.

And I always acknowledged his effort. I didn't want him to stop. I could cook a few things, but it wasn't really my jam. And when I did, I got more complaints than anything.

I'd rather build shit like the bridge we were working on down at the creek.

"What are you cooking, Bro?" Theo asked, pulling the lid off a large simmering pot.

Colton grabbed the lid from his brother. "Get out of here. It's a stew, but I also made a version for your vegetarian ass."

Theo beamed. It wasn't easy being the only vegetarian in a houseful of meat-eating mountain men.

"Beer, Theo?" I asked.

He patted his stomach. "No thanks. I'm cutting back on alcohol in preparation for my annual meditation retreat.

Oh right. Theo's retreat. He did it every year, and every year he tried to get Colton and me to join him.

So far, he hadn't succeeded.

Another one of his hippie tendencies, I liked to tease.

"You know," I said, looking between the two brothers, "I don't know that I've ever seen such polar opposite human beings. To think you're brothers is seriously baffling."

Colton brought a taste of the stew to his lips, closed his eyes, and smiled. It wasn't the first time he'd heard something like that.

Colton was a hardened, ex-military man who'd seen the world. He didn't say much, and was permanently scarred by a shattering heartbreak. I wouldn't be surprised if he never had another relationship in his life. By contrast, Theo had lived on the mountain all his life, and while he was strong as hell, was probably one of the gentlest human beings I'd ever known. He brought home injured animals all the time and somehow succeeded in nursing them back to health. In fact, I think there was a baby squirrel in a cage in his bedroom at that very moment.

Theo laughed. "Yeah, you should hear our mother talk. After all these years, she's still mystified that she gave birth to the two of us."

"Seriously. You're the burly carnivore, Colton, and Theo's the meditating vegetarian."

Theo nodded. "Yup. And we somehow manage to keep from beating the crap out of each other."

I didn't have any brothers, and living with two was an eye-opener. They bickered like old ladies but were wickedly loyal. Try to hurt one of them and you'd definitely have to deal with the wrath of the other.

Actually, try to hurt any of the three of us and you'd face the wrath of the rest of us. That was how close we'd grown.

We finally sat down to dinner. I was goddamn hungry, and so was everyone else, evidenced by the silence as we stuffed our faces.

"This is some good stuff, Colt," I said, digging in.

"The veg stew is all right, too," Theo added.

Colton took a swig of his beer and set it down on the rough-hewn dining table I'd built by hand. When you were up on the mountain, you had a good bit of time for such projects, something I never had when I was living a more conventional life.

"I'm thinking Bo should be back from Florida by now. What do you say we go over to visit him soon?" Colton suggested.

"Shit, have two months gone by already?" I asked. We liked to check in on our cool old neighbor whenever we could.

Colton nodded. "Yeah. Can you believe it. And what a bitch of a winter it was."

"Seriously, Bro," Theo said. "The bridge over the creek is nothing more than splinters. I hope the posts are still solid, or we'll be digging holes and pouring concrete to hold new ones."

I laughed. "Fucking Bo, getting out of town for the worst of the winter. Didn't he go down to Key West for some body painting festival?"

Colton slapped his hand on the table. "Holy shit, I forgot all about that. That old fucker gets more babes than any other man I know. And he's got to be in his late seventies. He must use a shitload of Viagra."

Theo nodded, wearing an electrified grin. "Hey, get this. Before he left for Florida, he asked me where he could get his pubes waxed."

I almost choked on my dinner. "No fucking way. What'd you tell him?"

He shrugged. "I told him I knew nothing about that sort of thing. Guess I've been on the mountain for too long, but I didn't know guys did that sort of thing. Can you imagine, getting your private parts waxed?"

"Women do it," Colton said.

"Crazy shit." Theo laughed.

4

———

LOGAN MEYER

"Happy birthday, Dad."

There was silence on the other end of the line, followed by a deep breath. "Hello, Logan."

Well. It was clear things hadn't changed much since I'd last spoken to the old man. Which was probably exactly a year ago today.

Normally, when I called, my mother answered. Which was how I preferred it.

"Did you have a good birthday, Dad? Mom bake your favorite cake?"

How she put up with such a tyrant of a man had always been beyond me.

My relationship with my father had been good for several years, primarily because we were working together and I deferred to him, not because I couldn't make my own decisions, but because it was the best way to keep the peace.

But a crisis that ended in the closing of our company put my relationship right back to square one—pretty much non-existent. In spite of my efforts to repair things.

"Chocolate cake," he said flatly.

Okay. He wasn't going to chat.

"All right, Dad. Wanted to let you know I was thinking about you on your birthday."

There was silence. "Thank you," he said after a moment.

And that was that.

Why did I even try? I supposed because the rift between Dad and me had worn so heavily on my mother that I vowed to keep trying, at least for as long as she was alive.

I was doing it for her. Because if I were honest with myself, my dad didn't deserve to have a relationship with me.

And yet, I kept trying. Crazy family shit.

Okay, and maybe it wasn't only for my mother. There was a heaving dose of guilt floating about.

When I was just out of college, I'd joined my father's construction company, and when he got a contract to build a huge residential subdivision, he put me in charge of it. A colossal fuck up on my part—unintentional, but still—that involved working with a shady subcontractor got the company in big trouble. First, we faced bankruptcy, then had to completely close. It had been devastating for us all, and my dad was never going to forgive me.

The man didn't have it in him.

The way it happened was pretty simple, which was probably what made it that much more insidious. I'd hired a company that used sub-par piping in their plumbing. I had no idea whether they'd done that before, but they royally fucked over my dad and me, and we ended up being sued by the home owners. I couldn't blame them.

We lost the most important asset we had—our reputation. All the work that had been pouring in slowed to a trickle and eventually dried up. Everything was liquidated in what was pretty much a fire sale, and my dad had barely said two words to me since.

Which was fine, really. He'd always been an ass and was still insufferably so.

That's when Colton, who I knew through mutual friends, had invited me to join Theo and him in the mountains. The brothers, living in the house where they'd grown up, needed someone with my skills and, more importantly, thought I'd be easy to get along with. I figured what the hell, I'd give it a shot until I decided what I wanted to do next. Which wasn't going to be easy because all I knew was how to build shit.

I'd loved the mountain since day one, the lack of women notwithstanding, and still had no plans to leave. We pretty much supported ourselves with hunting and fishing, and doing small jobs around the mountain. So far, I hadn't had to touch the small amount of savings I had, which made me very happy.

The lack of women was probably the only downside, which made the woman in the VW driving up the mountain all the more remarkable. I couldn't imagine where she'd been headed, especially since she'd been so cagey about it—and there sure as hell was no 'new motel' as she'd claimed.

She must have thought I was a freaking idiot to try that one on me.

But really. Where *had* she been going? And why was she so poorly prepared? People didn't randomly drive up this side of Deep Water Mountain for a nice day in the country. It was remote and unwelcoming.

Whatever. I'd never see her again.

I thanked Colton for dinner and said goodnight to everyone. I needed a good night's rest. Rebuilding the bridge over the creek that connected our property to Bo's was going to be a big-ass job, and I wanted to get on it early. And if Bo were back in town, I'd reward myself by bringing a six pack over to his place to hear about his undoubtedly crazy winter in Key West. His stories were legendary.

He was just that kind of guy.

5

AVA STONE

Now that it was daylight, it was painfully clear that Uncle Bo's cabin was about as bad as I'd thought it was in the dark.

Maybe even more so. If that were possible.

Perhaps the best way to deal with the place would be to drop a lit match in the middle of it and walk away.

After a night of bad dreams, I sat straight up in bed and looked around his room for the first time in full daylight. The floor was covered in rough, unfinished boards that I didn't dare walk on in bare feet, and his cracked bedroom window had so many cobwebs on it, I could barely see through it.

But the funny thing was, I'd slept well. Like, really

well. Even though I'd crashed with my clothes on, about as depressed as I'd been in a really long time.

The cabin had electricity, thank god. But that didn't mean Bo had availed himself of the opportunity to properly illuminate his home with modern fixtures. No, there was one bare bulb hanging from the ceiling of his bedroom that in the dark provided just enough light to cast shadows and scare the shit out of a city girl like myself.

I'd slept in my clothes. Sure, I'd brought my organic cotton PJs, but I wasn't about to rifle through my duffel bag and spread out when I couldn't see what other creatures I might be sharing my room with.

I groaned with discomfort because I'd not even removed my underwire bra and took a look at the bed I'd just slept in. Damn if he didn't have soft one hundred percent cotton sheets, firm pillows, and a fluffy down comforter.

Bizarre.

What was a man who didn't even have indoor plumbing doing with such nice bedding?

Yup, there was no indoor plumbing. Which I must have blocked from my childhood memory of the place. Or maybe when I was ten, I simply didn't care that there was an outhouse in the backyard.

After my long drive up, of course I had to pee. I'd entered the house, the key the attorney had given me useless because the lock on the front door *didn't even work*, and ran like a maniac looking for the toilet.

Surprise! There was none. I opened every door in the

place, not that there were that many, and because I was desperate, I ran outside and peed on the side of the house. That's when I noticed, while squatting, a couple outbuildings, and got a sinking feeling that one of them was to be my bathroom.

No wonder my mother stopped bringing us up here.

How would I ever sell this place to anyone other than a crazy, eccentric mountain man? Were there even that many of them out there? And would my real estate agent be able to find one?

As soon as I was done peeing, I took a look at the outside of the house, still lit up due to my headlights. I wanted to be positive. I really did. But the front porch was propped up on big river rocks, and one of the front steps was broken through. The roof of the porch sagged, and the wooden boards on the outside of the house were shredded in spots, like they'd rotted. I wanted to Google a picture of rotted wood, but had to wander around until my phone got a signal. And big surprise, there was no internet access.

Because of course.

As soon as I could, I called my mother.

"Mom?" I said, my voice wavering.

"Ava, honey. Are you up at Bo's? Is it like you remembered?"

Ugh. Where to start.

"Not exactly, Mom. It's a bit more... rustic."

"Honey, it was always rustic."

"But Mom, I didn't remember an outdoor bathroom. Did you?"

She laughed. "Of course, I remember that. Why do you think we stopped going up there? At one point I even offered him the money to build a real bathroom, but he said he was fine with what he had. He was a bit of an odd bird, Ava."

She wasn't kidding.

"The house is in pretty bad shape, Mom. I'm not sure what I can do with it. Maybe sell it as is."

"That might be the best way to do. See what the realtor says before you make any decisions."

"I don't have the money to do everything that needs to be done here." Saying the words out loud dropped my spirits to a new low. I'd had such high hopes about how a windfall of cash from selling Bo's place might put me on track to buy a place for myself at home. I had about five thousand hard-earned bucks in the bank, which had once made me feel rich. Now it was dawning on me how little it was, facing the kind of renovations that would be needed to make Bo's place habitable.

Shit, shit, shit.

"The house is gross, Mom."

"Can you go to a hotel for the few days you're up there?" she asked.

Yeah. The new motel I tried to convince that guy of yesterday.

"There's no motel, Mom. I'm in the middle of nowhere. But you know what's weird?"

I hesitated telling her because it seemed gossipy. Even though Uncle Bo had laid a turd on me with his rickety cabin, I felt a modicum of loyalty toward him for doing his best to hook me up. But in the end, I dished.

"Mom, he has a five-thousand-dollar bed. And super nice linens. Is that not the strangest thing?"

I knew because I Googled Duxiana, some fancy-schmancy luxury bed brand. It actually cost more than five thousand bucks, something I wouldn't expect living-off-the-land Bo to spend his money on.

I mean, who has a five-thousand-dollar bed but no indoor plumbing?

What in the actual fuck?

"You know honey, he had his priorities. And from what I knew, he was very popular with the ladies. Maybe that's where he thought he ought to upgrade."

Gross. He'd bed women and then expect them to pee in an outhouse?

"Listen, hon," Mom said, "I'm heading out for tennis. Keep me posted okay? Sounds like so much fun."

Had she heard a word I'd said? I was in crisis thanks to *her* brother, and she was skipping off to tennis.

"Okay, Mom. Love you."

"Love you too, Ava!"

6

AVA STONE

I WAS MAKING A LIST OF EVERYTHING I COULD SEE THAT needed to be done with the cabin because I was a project manager after all, and no one loved a spreadsheet more than I did. But when I heard a truck barreling down the lane toward the house, I snapped my laptop shut and grabbed my pepper spray.

Oh. It was the contractor I'd called.

I walked out on the front porch to greet him.

"You must be Pete," I said, shaking hands.

"Damn. It's been a while since I've been here," he said, taking it all in. "Your uncle and I used to have a running poker game. All the guys loved coming over here. No wife or other women to contend with and tell us to smoke outside or keep our noise down."

Great. I was happy for him. Maybe he'd want to buy the place from me.

"Any word on how old Bo died?" he asked.

I would normally be surprised at such an indelicate question, but since arriving at a place with no toilet, it seemed typical niceties would have be out of place anyway.

"Um, not sure. Something happened to him in Florida. He'd gone down to Key West to get away from the winter."

He fake-smacked the side of his head. "Oh, that's right. Lucky bastard."

"Yeah." I nodded, staring at the busted-through front step.

Pete could feel my pain. "I've been here many a time, but I will say that Bo really let the place go in the last couple years."

You figure?

He ran his fingers along the posts holding up the porch and peered around the side of the house to get a look at the rest of it. "You got some real bad dry rot here."

Thank you, Google.

He pulled a small notepad out of his pocket and began scribbling. "And I haven't even seen the inside yet," he enthusiastically added.

"The biggest problem is that there is no bathroom."

The more I thought about it, the more I was pissed that Uncle Bo had left this place to me. It was more like he'd dumped a pile of crap on me. Instead of thinking I was a cool niece who deserved his assets, he must have thought I was a neglectful relative whom he could torment from beyond the grave.

I tagged after Pete for nearly an hour as he picked apart the cabin, listing everything that needed to be done on his notepad. He only stopped when he ran out of paper.

I was fucked. Completely and totally fucked.

He took a deep breath. "It's not looking good, Ava. Unless you have deep pockets, you might just want to sell this place at a fire sale and pocket what you can."

So much for my new condo.

I looked over his list, trying not to cry. "Pete, what are the top five things that most need to be done? Like if it were your place, where would you start?"

He scratched his head. "Obviously, the front porch. And then the roof."

He hadn't even mentioned a bathroom. You know you're in bad shape when actually installing a toilet is not at the top of the list of things a house needs.

"The roof? I guess, then, that those are for catching rain?" I asked, pointing at two random buckets in the living room.

"Yup."

Can you un-inherit something? Like could I call the attorney and tell him I didn't want what Bo had left me?

I could always change my phone number.

"All right, Pete. Can you work up a quote for each thing that needs to be done so I can pick and choose if it comes down to that?"

"Sure thing."

He left, leaving me to wallow in self-pity, his pick-up truck competently navigating the rutted road leading to the cabin. I sank onto the front steps, avoiding the stair with the busted through plank, and put my head in my hands.

I'd taken time off work and driven up to this godforsaken mountain, apparently for nothing.

That would teach me to head into a situation with dollar signs in my eyes. I'd probably attracted bad karma or something.

That's when I heard noise coming from the woods. I jumped up and ran inside, leaving the door open a crack to peek out and see what it was.

I was pretty sure they had bears and mountain lions on Deep Water, and I wasn't sure my pepper spray would do much against them. But I patted my pocket where I'd tucked it, just in case.

Then I heard the noise again. It didn't sound like an animal, but more like some sort of starting and stopping machine. Wild animals didn't make sounds like that, did they?

I ditched my designer boots and slipped into my sneakers, venturing back outside. When I'd identified the direction the noise was coming from, I stealthily started moving toward it. The property, which was pretty much cleared except for the occasional tree or bush, bumped up to thick woods, too dense to see more than a few feet into.

The sounds continued and a voice carried over them.

Holy crap. There was a person out there. A man. But I couldn't tell what he was saying.

After some poking around, I identified an overgrown path leading in the direction of the commotion. The tree branches and leaves had grown wild, but the dirt path was well worn. I started down it as noiselessly as I could.

As I progressed, the sounds got louder. Someone seemed to be building something, occasionally talking to someone else who was not responding. As I rounded a corner, I could see a feral-looking man chopping at what looked like a broken-down bridge crossing the creek.

I vaguely remembered a creek from my childhood visits, but not a bridge. Had there been one then?

The guy, in a tattered plaid flannel shirt and long hair spilling out of a loose ponytail, was talking to himself.

Oh my god. I'd come across a bona fide crazy mountain man.

Shit. I couldn't understand his mumbling. Maybe he didn't even speak English.

Time to exit.

But when I did, my foot slipped in the mud. I tumbled off the path and down a small hill, heading straight for the creek.

Thinking fast, I grabbed a branch to stop my descent and pulled myself back up onto the trail. With a glance back at the guy, who'd heard me and was now totally watching, I took off, hightailing it for the cabin. Since the front door didn't lock, I pushed the kitchen table against it and then backed the sofa up against that. It wouldn't keep out anyone who really wanted in, but it would at least slow them down until I could find a better weapon than my pepper spray.

Digging through the kitchen cupboards, I found a big knife in a leather sheath. I held it close and sat down on the sofa, which was holding the table, which was blocking the door.

I was ready.

7

———

THEO PAYNE

WHAT THE HELL WAS THAT?

Or should I say *who* the hell was that?

Unless my eyes were playing tricks on me, I'd just seen a woman in a red fleece jacket fall down the creek embankment, pull herself back out, and take off like a kid who'd been caught doing something bad.

I crossed over the creek using the wobbly log I'd laid over it while the bridge was under construction, and scrambled to where the woman had been. Sure enough, there were flattened leaves and branches where she'd wiped out.

So, I hadn't imagined it.

It was Bo's property she was on. Maybe he'd returned

from Florida and this was one of his latest women? She seemed pretty young for a guy who's seventy-plus, but you never knew about the man.

But hell, who knew what he was up to? He got more pussy than all three men in my house put together.

Yeah, Bo was that kind of guy. Everybody loved him. He could spin a tale that lasted for hours. People just wanted to be around him, and that included women.

We were pretty friendly with Bo, getting together on occasion for beers and when we were feeling extravagant, some nice scotch. We also kept an eye out for him, given his advanced age and propensity for living large. That was part of the reason that, after each winter, we rebuilt the bridge over the creek that abutted his property. Going the long way around was a hell of a walk, and besides, if we cut through his land, we could reach the fishing pond in minutes.

"Hey. What are you doing up there?" Logan called, his arms full of more bridge-building materials.

"Oh, hey." I waved at him from the opposite side of the creek, and started making my way back down to cross over and get back to work.

"Dude, the strangest thing. There was a woman up there," I said, pointing. "She saw me and ran off like a bat out of hell."

Logan frowned. "What? On Bo's property?"

"Yeah."

"Do you think it was someone he brought home? Or someone who shouldn't be there?"

I shrugged. "I have no idea. I'll go on up there a bit later."

Logan started screwing the boards that would make the bridge's handrail. We'd done this a few years in a row now, each winter's storms having ripped out the previous year's bridge.

What would be really efficient would be to build a bridge big enough to withstand the winter snowfall.

But what would be the fun in that? We liked building shit. All three of us did.

Logan stopped working and looked up at me, running his hand over his bald head. "What did she look like?"

I looked up. "Who?"

He rolled his eyes. "The woman. The woman you saw in the woods just now. What did she look like?"

Hmmm. Good question. "I only saw her for a second before she took off. But she was wearing a red jacket, and had dark hair in a ponytail."

"Was she pretty?"

I wracked my memory as best I could. "You know, I can't say. What I did see of her was a blur. Why?"

"I wonder if she had something to do with the woman I saw yesterday—the one who ran out of gas. I mean we've had sightings of two women we don't know in the last two days."

I shooed away his concern. "Eh, you're thinking too hard about this. I'm sure it's nothing."

He shrugged and got back to work while I tried to remember what I could about her. But she'd run off too fast.

And why? Was she not supposed to be there?

Fucking weird. We didn't see strangers around here. It was part of what made our side of the mountain so appealing. You could disappear and not be bothered by anyone.

Maybe that's what she was trying to do?

8

THEO PAYNE

I DIDN'T WANT TO ALARM LOGAN ANY MORE THAN I already had. Like my brother, his first instinct was to think the worst when something was out of the ordinary. I guess lives like theirs will do that to you. I, on the other hand, grew up on Deep Water Mountain and had never lived anywhere else. It was a pretty peaceful place and not a lot of shit went on. If I saw someone I didn't know, I introduced myself.

It's funny what getting off the mountain will do to you. My brother Colton left shortly after high school and joined the military. When he returned four years later, he, like Logan, was more wary about the people around us. I couldn't say what was better or worse. They were street wise in a way I supposed I was not. But I could drop a line in the pond and in an hour have enough fish for all of us for dinner.

They couldn't do that.

We each brought something to the table.

When Logan finished for the day, he headed back up to the house to wash for dinner. I told him I'd follow shortly. Because the bridge wasn't done yet, I scrambled across the log bridging both sides of the creek, and scrambled up the embankment on the other side.

I wanted to know who the hell that woman was, if she was still around.

The path to Bo's was short, about ten minutes from our door to his. It didn't take me long to reach the end of the woods where his property clearing started. And as I suspected, there was a light on in the cabin.

Was Bo back? And if so, did he have company?

I walked around the side of the house. It didn't look much changed since I'd checked on it a couple weeks ago. We didn't know exactly when he'd be back from Florida because Bo always kept his options open. But, the weather was getting warmer now, and he could be expected any day.

I turned the corner and was now in the front of the house.

I was not expecting what I saw.

There sat a VW Bug. In bright red.

What the...?

Hadn't Logan just talked about a VW Bug?

Like he'd given gasoline to a woman in a VW Bug?

And even stranger, Bo's truck was nowhere to be seen.

What was going on?

Only one way to find out.

I walked up the dilapidated front steps of Bo's house and found the front door unlatched. I pushed it open and walked right in.

Only to be greeted by a shriek that must have been heard across the damn mountain.

"Who are you?" a woman screamed, grabbing a too-small towel to cover her privates.

Yup. She was butt naked. As in undressed. Completely.

Standing at the kitchen sink, giving herself a sponge bath.

The fuck?

If this was one of Bo's new women, I had to hand it to the guy. She was hot as shit. Curves for days, smooth olive skin, and dark eyes that were currently giving me a deadly stink eye.

And young, at least for his old ass.

I averted my gaze. Slightly. "Where's Bo?" I demanded.

"He… he's dead. Now who the hell are you? No, never mind. Get out of my house."

Her house?

My gaze went back to her, where she was unsuccessfully covering herself. She'd managed to obscure her crotch area and one tit, but the other was hanging out for the world to see. I wasn't telling her until I knew what was going on.

"Wait a minute," I said, ignoring her questions, "he's dead? When? How?"

Bo was *dead?*

It couldn't be.

He'd been old, no denying that, but to think he was gone was… inconceivable. He'd been more alive than most people I'd met in my life.

Had he been sick?

Was it an accident?

Was he alone?

For a second, a lump choked my throat, but I swallowed that shit right away. And fortunately, my voice returned. "Who are *you* and what are *you* doing here?"

"I'm his niece. I inherited the property."

Wow. Just wow. She sure didn't look like the owner of a mountain cabin.

I held my hands up as a peace offering. "I'm a neighbor. We saw each other in the woods earlier today."

I wanted to ask why the hell she ran away, but I figured I'd tackle one thing at a time. Like what she was going to do with the cabin.

And just when I was about to, there was a knock on the partially-open front door. My old buddy Pete stuck his head in.

"Heya!" he called.

The woman shrieked again, this time darting to the back of the house, holding the skimpy towel as she ran, her round ass jiggling.

"Theo. What're you doing here?" Pete asked. "And why is Ava… naked?"

We watched her slam the bedroom door shut.

"I guess she was bathing at the sink. I saw that someone was here and made the mistake of walking in because the door was partially open. I actually don't know her name, but she told me Bo passed away."

He nodded. "Yup. That's right. Old Bo is gone, and that's his niece Ava. I met with her yesterday about doing some work on the place."

I looked around. *Some* work was an understatement.

"When did Bo pass? And how did it happen?"

Pete shrugged. "I don't know. I don't think Ava knows."

Damn. I had a sudden urge to get out of there. I'd done what I'd set out to do—find out who was lurking in the woods and whether that someone was with Bo. I didn't need any more than that.

"Good luck," I said, gesturing toward the bedroom and lowering my voice. "She seems like a handful."

Pete patted me on the back and I took off. I would have liked to tell Ava I enjoyed... meeting her, but I wasn't sticking around. Bo was gone and it didn't feel right.

I BURST INTO THE HOUSE. "Guys, guys. I have some news about Bo."

Colton and Logan looked my way as I joined them in the living room.

"Bo has... passed away." I could barely believe the words as I spoke them.

My brother's jaw dropped, and Logan, after staring at me for a moment, put his head in his hands. And now that I was out of Bo's house and had settled the matter of who the woman in red was, I could absorb the news, too.

I plopped into an easy chair and stared at the floor.

Colton recovered first. "Holy shit. What... happened? Do you know?"

I shook my head. "No idea. I went over to the house when I saw a strange woman in the woods and found out she was his niece who had inherited the place."

Logan's head snapped up. "She didn't have a VW, did she?"

I pointed at Logan. "*Yes*. Same woman you helped. At least I guess so. How many women are up here on the mountain with red VWs?"

He pressed his lips together and nodded. "Wow. Just wow. We've lost Bo and gained a princess."

Might as well share the whole story.

I leaned forward in my seat. "Guys, that's not all. I walked in on her bathing at the kitchen sink. Naked."

Logan looked up at the ceiling and laughed. "Oh my god, that's right, Bo doesn't have a bathroom. She must have shit blue pickles over that."

"But, dude, you saw her naked? You just walked in on her?" Colton asked.

I knew where my brother was going with this. "Yup. Scared the shit out of her. Bo never had his lock fixed, and the door was partially open. How was I to know she'd be standing right there, soaping herself up."

Colton chuckled. "That's crazy. So what's she look like?"

And there it was. My horn dog brother.

I stole a look at Logan, who rolled his eyes.

"She was hot, Colt. Even beautiful. Why don't you go over there right now and see for yourself?"

The bastard actually looked at his watch. He'd had his heart broken into a million pieces awhile back and would probably never date again, but he was still a horn dog.

"Nah. Too late. Tomorrow, though…"

I couldn't blame Colton for wanting to check her out. And to be honest, I planned to do the same again, too.

9

AVA STONE

So, not only had my neighbor seen me butt-ass naked, but so had my contractor.

What a winner. I was making good impressions all around. I knew two people on Deep Water Mountain, and they'd both seen my bare ass.

As if it wasn't bad enough that I had to bathe at the goddamn kitchen sink, people in these parts didn't seem to know about knocking before entering someone's home. The first thing I was going to do was have a huge deadbolt put on Bo's front door so that couldn't happen again. Maybe I'd even have a doorbell installed.

But what was I talking about? I wasn't staying here any longer than I had to.

I ate another one of my energy bars and sipped some

wine. It was a disgusting combination but I hadn't figured out where the general store was to do some shopping. And as I enjoyed my dinner, I looked over the estimate from the contractor, Pete.

The cheap version of what he could do was fifty thousand dollars. The high end was one hundred.

I didn't have fifty thousand dollars, so I sure as hell didn't have one hundred thousand.

Shit, shit, shit.

I was so in over my head.

I could put part of the work on my credit card—the one that wasn't yet maxed out. But that would only get me so far.

I did have one other idea.

My neighbor—the one who saw me naked—seemed pretty adept at the tools he'd been using down in the creek. Maybe he'd be available for some work, if his rates were more reasonable than Pete's.

I pulled some of Bo's clothes on, cinching up his work pants with a belt and dressing in one of his flannel shirts. My designer jeans and cashmere sweaters were not going to cut it this time.

I headed back to the path I'd taken earlier, hoping I could catch the guy who'd walked in on me bathing.

Too late. He was no longer there.

Shit.

I could see he was building a bridge for crossing the creek. But why did he need a way to cross to Bo's property? As the new owner, I needed to get to the bottom of that.

For the time being, there was a ten-or-so-foot log spanning the creek, which must have been how he crossed when he'd come over the day before. I suspected it would lead to him, so I bushwhacked my way down the embankment, gingerly stepping on it to see how stable it was.

So far so good.

If the log was strong enough to hold a guy, it would certainly hold me. I slowly put one foot in front of the other, praying I wouldn't slip. The log was strong, as I suspected, but what I didn't realize until I was in the middle of it was that it wasn't secured on either end. Depending on where I placed my weight, it rolled a little with each step. Not a good time to figure something like that out. I glanced over my shoulder to see if where I'd started was any closer than where I was going.

Not really.

Onward.

I focused on the end a few feet ahead of me, picking up speed. And because that's just how my life was working out, the log shifted when I was one step away from the end. Before I could jump for the embankment, it sent me flying.

Because of course.

I was now in slow-moving but very cold water to my knees and facing a wall of dirt nearly my height to crawl back out. I looked back to where I'd started from, and the embankment on that side was even higher.

The best part was that it was starting to get dark.

God, I was a fucking loser.

I dug my fingers into the dirt and crawled my way up until I'd heaved myself over the edge. I lay there a moment while I caught my breath, soaked and covered in gritty mud.

And then I heard gunshots.

I couldn't get a damn break.

The sound reverberated, making it hard to know where it was coming from. But when it got closer, I knew I had to do something.

I got to my feet and began to run toward a path I'd spotted. It was unfortunately leading me farther from Bo's property, but I didn't know who the hell was shooting guns, and I wasn't about to sit around and wait to find out.

Bridge-building guy must be around somewhere.

But what the fuck? Guns in the woods? I occasionally heard guns at home in the crappy neighborhood where I lived, but on Deep Water Mountain? Give me a break.

Luckily, as soon as I started down the path in my soaked and muddy clothing, I saw a plume of smoke, presumably from a fireplace, and when I got closer, I saw the house it was coming from.

In the front window, I could see the guy who'd barged in on me earlier. The ponytail guy who'd been building the bridge.

Oh, thank god.

But what if he were one of the shooters?

My mind was made up when another gunshot rang. Charging up the house's steps, I pounded on the front door. When it flew open, I threw myself into the man's arms.

Yup. The same guy who'd seen me naked.

But at the moment, that didn't matter. Survival was all I could think about.

"Oh, thank god you're here," I cried, pushing my way inside. "Please help me. There is some homicidal maniac out there shooting guns."

He peeled my arms off and stepped back, taking in my soaked jeans and sneakers and the mud that covered the rest of me.

And then, as if my life weren't already a freakshow along the lines of *The Twilight Zone*, who stood behind him but the guy who'd helped fill my empty tank of gas on the side of the road.

Was this a bad joke? Because it sure felt like one.

It might have been from running or the adrenaline, but I was suddenly searing hot and the room started to move. It became hard to breathe, as if someone were sitting on my chest. I sank to my knees right there on the floor, worried about whether or not I was going to vomit, and the room went black.

10

COLTON PAYNE

"Jesus. What the hell's going on here?"

When I arrived home from a fruitless hunting effort due to some noisy idiot in the woods, I nearly fell over the body of a wet and muddy woman slumped in our doorway.

What the fuck?

Logan and Theo stared at her, their mouths hanging open.

I knelt to check her pulse, something I knew to do from my Army days.

"That... that would be Bo's niece," my brother stammered. "Her name is Ava."

Why was she on our floor, hopefully nothing more than just passed out?

Her pulse was strong, thank god, and when I pushed her hair off her face, her eyes started to flutter open. Good sign.

"Hey, will one of you grab her a glass of water?" I asked, gesturing toward the kitchen.

Snapping out of his surprise, Logan hustled to the sink and filled a glass. "She just showed up at the door, screaming that someone was shooting at her."

Oh, for Christ's sake. She was the one in the woods.

Logan continued. "She's also the woman I helped who'd run out of gas. Fucking bizarre," he mumbled, rubbing a hand over his bald head.

So, the woman Logan gave gas to was on her way up here to check out Bo's place, which she'd inherited because he'd died.

That part made sense.

But what didn't was why she was on our floor, unconscious. Or rather, coming to.

As if he could read my mind, Theo answered my question as I propped her up and put water to her lips. "Dude. She thought someone was after her with a gun."

"Theo, she's probably talking about me. Do you think she might have heard a *shotgun*?"

People unfamiliar with firearms rarely knew the differences among guns. One sounded similar to the others and from the looks of this woman, although she was wearing outdoor clothing, her sleek hair and painted nails gave away that she might be new to the world of firearms.

My jaw tightened with irritation. "Guys, if she heard a

shotgun, then she probably heard mine. I was working on getting a deer when someone went running and screaming through the woods and ruined my shot."

She suddenly jerked awake, spilling the water I was trying to give her. "Wh… where am I?" she murmured.

Theo knelt down in front of her. "Hey. Do you remember me? Building the bridge? We um… met yesterday when you…"

She looked at him, frowning.

Yeah, she remembered him.

He took her dirty hand and patted it. "I'm Theo. You're Ava, right?"

She wriggled out of my hold, leaving me covered with her mud, and looked around. "What happened? Did I faint?"

I stood and backed away from her. She didn't seem like the most stable person. But my brother, the always kind–hearted Theo, remained in front of her, kneeling.

"You came running in our door because you heard a gun. Then you fainted. Are you feeling better?"

She nodded. "Yeah. I think so."

"Theo stood and extended his hand. "Come have a seat. I don't imagine the floor is that comfortable."

"Theo, she's filthy—"

He raised his hand at me indicating he wasn't going to listen, no matter what. Fine. He could clean up her mess later.

And how the hell had she gotten that way? Had jumped in the creek? I'd seen city folk do some stupid things up here on Deep Water Mountain, but not many of them waded through a creek fully clothed when the sun was going down.

"Ava, this is my brother, Colton, and that's Logan, who I think helped you when you ran out of gas the other day."

She looked us over again, suspicious as hell, but finally nodded. She let Theo lead her to one of our dining chairs.

The dining chairs Logan and I had made. By hand. Last summer. That we tried to take good care of.

I shot my brother the stink eye. He ignored it.

She looked at us with wide eyes, her gaze settling on my shotgun. "Why do you have a gun? Was that you shooting out there? I... I didn't know who or what it was."

I put the gun away in the armoire near the door and took a seat opposite her. "I was hunting. For our dinner. I bring home meat every week." I gestured at my camo pants and bright orange vest, but the symbolism was lost on her.

"You were hunting? Like, animals?" she said sheepishly.

"What did you think the shots were?" Theo asked.

She blushed. "At home I live in a not-so-great neigh-borhood. Gunshots there are not people hunting for their dinner." She laughed weakly.

I had to admit, she had a point about being scared. When I first returned home from the Middle East and returned to Deep Water Mountain, it took some time to get used to hearing the gunshots of hunters. Each one took me back to my combat missions.

Actually, sometimes they still did.

"Ava, I'm sorry to have scared you. But people in the

mountains hunt. Sometimes they use shotguns, sometimes they use bows and arrows."

She winced at *bows and arrows*.

And I had to say that, even though she had initially
come off as a lunatic and was clearly wearing someone
else's too-big clothes, she was quite attractive.

"Well, aren't I just the big freaking idiot?" she
mumbled.

Did she want us to answer that? Because we would…

Logan joined us at the dining table. "Ava, why did you
tell me you were going to a hotel the other day? I might
add, an *imaginary hotel*."

He looked at me, and I bit my lip to keep from laughing. Theo ignored us.

"Could I have some more water, please?" she asked,
holding up her empty glass.

She looked down at her filthy hands, bits of hair falling
around her face as if she wanted to hide behind it. She
was embarrassed. I would be, too.

She finally looked up, directly at Logan, her eyes defiant. Guess she was getting her mojo back. "Yes, I lied. I'm
sorry. But I didn't know who you were. Any woman
would have done the same. You know, I was going to my
uncle's cabin, where I'd be alone. I didn't want a stranger
to know that. Shit, he doesn't even have a lock on the
front door."

Her hand flew to her mouth and she squeezed her eyes
shut at her admission.

Theo to the rescue, again. "Look, Ava, we were friends
with Bo. You can relax."

She stood, looking at the footprints leading from our front door. "I'm sorry about the mess. If you have a rag, I'll clean it up."

What the hell good would that do if she were still wet and muddy?

And had she really thought we were thugs running loose in the woods?

I didn't want to be an asshole, but the sooner she left Deep Water, the better. This chick was trouble.

I tried to hide my irritation. I really did. But the more I thought about how the night's dinner was ruined, the more pissed I got.

"We have no meat for dinner tonight. I was looking forward to a nice backstrap or tenderloin."

Theo shot me a look. He didn't give a shit. He was a vegetarian. "Relax. I can make fish for dinner. And maybe Ava would like to join us."

No. Please tell me my brother had not just gone off the deep end.

I'd be having a word with him later.

But Ava wasn't stupid. She saw the look on my face and shook her head. "Thanks. No. I'm not dressed for dinner."

Theo held his hands up. "Problem solved. I have some clothes you can borrow. Looks like what you're wearing isn't yours, anyway."

She looked down. "Yeah. These are Bo's things."

"You'll join us, then?"

She looked at Theo, then Logan and me, and shrugged. "Okay. I will. Thank you."

11

—

COLTON PAYNE

AVA EMERGED FROM THE BACK OF THE HOUSE WEARING A pair of Theo's hippie drawstring pants and a loose tunic. The mud she'd been covered with was gone, and she actually had a smile on her face.

"Thank you so much for inviting me. It's so nice to know Bo had good neighbors."

I handed her a beer.

Was she going to want a glass? Because she wasn't going to get one.

"Thanks, Colton. God, I haven't had a beer in ages." She took a big chug and smacked her lips. "Mmmm. So good."

"Why don't you drink beer if you like it?"

She shrugged one shoulder. "Carbs, I guess. I'm always worried about carbs. Isn't everyone worried about carbs?"

We just looked at her.

In what world were men worried about carbs?

Apparently, hers.

"Oh wow. What kind of fish is that?" she asked as Theo pulled his latest catch out of the fridge. "I love fish."

He unwrapped the paper and Ava's eyes bugged out.

Hadn't she ever seen a whole fish?

"It's brook trout. Tastes delicious. Wait till you try it. I'm gonna clean it now."

While they were becoming fast friends, I watched with amusement as Theo took a short knife, stuck it all the way up in the fish's underside, and slit it wide open.

Ava swallowed hard.

Running his fingers along the fish's insides, he scooped the guts out and put them in a small pile, shaking his hand to get the goo off, which resulted in spraying innards in Ava's direction.

With a larger knife, Theo then hacked the head off.

Ava's mouth dropped open.

"Now," he said proudly, "we wrap it up in foil and put it on the coals. When it's done and we take it out, the skin will peel right off, and it will be amazing."

Ava's color began to return. And apparently so did her power of conversation.

"Where are you all from?" she asked brightly, helping herself to another beer.

"Colton and I grew up right here in this house. Logan

is from down valley. You?" Theo asked, barely taking his eyes off her.

I had a feeling he'd be sweet on her.

"Oh, I'm from the city. Been there forever."

The city. Of course.

"Ava, how're you liking the mountains so far? You enjoying Deep Water?" Logan asked.

Her shoulders slumped, and she twisted her face. "Are you kidding? To begin with, I have no bathroom, which royally sucks. On top of that, I ran out of gas and you know, just fell in a creek. Those things were my fault of course, but they sure don't seem like good omens."

She shook her head hard.

"How 'bout we show you around sometime?" he offered.

She wrinkled her nose. "Show me around? What is there to see?" She gestured outside. "We're surrounded by woods. End of story. Right?"

Holy shit. The sooner this woman went back to *the city*, the better.

"Are you kidding?" I asked. "It's freaking beautiful up here, and the views you get hiking can take your breath away," I said.

She shrugged.

"And did you know there's a pond on Bo's property? That's where this fish came from, in fact."

Theo looked up at the sky. "Thank you, Bo, for this amazing fish."

"My point is, Ava, that you shouldn't knock it. This

area is beautiful, especially when you know what to look for."

Fidgeting in her seat, she looked unconvinced. "I don't know, Colton. The woods are dangerous. There's scary stuff out there."

I held my hands up. "Okay. Someone has been watching too much *Friday the 13th*."

Everyone burst out laughing.

"Fine, laugh all you want. But you'll be hard pressed to change my mind."

Sounded like a fun challenge, if you could put up with a pain in the ass.

SEVERAL BEERS LATER, and with a giant fish carcass picked clean in the middle of our table, we started sharing Bo stories.

"Geez. It's amazing. I know pretty much nothing about the guy," Ava said, throwing her hands up. "I mean, who would have thought such a crusty old guy would be such a chick magnet?"

Logan shook his head. "Seriously. I wouldn't have believed it if I hadn't seen it with my own eyes."

Ava leaned onto the table and lowered her voice like she had a big secret to share. "Get this. He has a very fancy, expensive bed. The man has no indoor bathroom, and yet has a five-thousand-dollar mattress."

We all fell back in our chairs, laughing.

"No fucking way," I said.

"I'm serious. The first night I slept on it, I was surprised how nice it was. I looked at the label and Googled it. Duxiana. Very high end."

"Oh my god." Logan laughed. "The man shits in the woods, but he has a nice place to take his women to bed."

Theo shook his head. "Guy knew what his priorities were, that's for damn sure."

I was going to miss him. "He had that cabin a long time. We grew up sneaking onto his property and getting into minor mischief, and he never got us in trouble. He was a cool guy." I actually felt a lump growing in my throat. Shit, I hadn't cried since the military.

"He'd give us his old Playboys, which we hid from Mom in the shed. One time she found them and wanted to know where we got them. But we never ratted Bo out." Theo laughed.

Ava looked like she was far away. "I'll never get to know him now that he's gone. It's too bad. He and my mom had some kind of falling out and we stopped seeing him. I don't even know what it was about, except that my mother didn't approve of his lifestyle."

I guess it was a matter of perspective. No one I knew, and that consisted mostly of people on Deep Water Mountain, had an issue with Bo's lifestyle. In fact, I think most people envied him and his *go for it* spirit.

"You know, Ava, I'm not sure you've missed your chance to know him," I said. "You're in his home and will be going through every belonging he had. You're going to get to know him, possibly even better than if he were still alive."

God knew what the hell she'd come across in that place. And what I wouldn't give to be a fly on the wall for that.

12

AVA STONE

HOLY SHIT. I JUST HAD DINNER WITH THREE HOT MOUNTAIN men.

And now, one of them was driving me home.

'Course I'd looked like absolute dogshit, actually worse than dogshit, drowning in Uncle Bo's too-big clothes, and then in Theo's hippie duds. And it didn't help that when I arrived, I was dripping wet and covered in mud. And then tracked it into their house.

Way *not* to make a good impression.

As we finished our after-dinner beers, I noticed a couple of the guys stifling yawns. While I wasn't in the least bit tired, I figured I'd better get out of their hair. I might not know the difference between street guns and hunting guns, but I did know when it was time to leave.

Besides, it's not like I'd actually been invited there to begin with, having showed up out of nowhere and then eaten their food.

And then there was Colton, who'd given me dirty looks practically the whole night for messing up his hunting. I couldn't blame him. It was amazing they'd invited me to break bread with them at all, when I was clearly still in pariah status.

But it was Theo who'd invited me, maybe because he'd seen me naked and considered us friends. Maybe he felt like he owed me something since I gave him a free show. And while his invite was sweet, it wouldn't have been so bad to basically turn around and head back home to ditch Bo's filthy clothes and give myself a nice sponge bath in the drafty kitchen.

Yeah, I was living the high life.

Honestly, I nearly *had* run out the door when Theo started gleefully gutting his fish. But I forced myself to stick around so I could change their mind about me. I wanted to prove that I might be a city girl, but I was still cool. Didn't take long to figure out it would take more than one dinner for that.

Yeah, mine was a winning move, pounding on their door for help, thinking a homicidal maniac was after me with a gun, when it was merely one of them out hunting meat for their dinner.

Which they'd missed out on, all because of me.

I didn't say anything, but personally, I was glad to have saved Bambi. It wasn't something a person got to do every day.

When I found the right time to make my exit, I jumped to my feet. "It's been great getting to know you all. I'm so grateful you are here."

Really. How lucky was I to have nice neighbors who also happened to be good looking, even if they didn't much care for me?

And truthfully, they really weren't just good looking.

They were positively beautiful. Like, perfect.

In a way I didn't even know was possible.

Theo and Colton looked alike with their dark eyes and dimples, and yet they were so opposite—one, gregarious and happy, the other sulking and grumpy. Simply looking at them could make your head spin, with Theo's hippie ponytail contrasted by Colton's preppy Ralph Lauren good looks.

And then there was Logan, the savior with the gas can, who I stole glances at while he drove me back home after dinner. His profile was flawlessly balanced with a strong brow and nose, and a head shaved so smoothly I could hardly keep my hands off it. While I couldn't see much in the streetlight-less mountain roads, the dashboard reflected enough light onto the steering wheel and his hands, which were enormous, like big, human-shaped shovels.

"I really appreciate the ride home, Logan," I said, holding the bag of wet, soiled clothes between my knees.

He turned up the drive to Bo's, his truck handling the rutted road a lot better than my VW. "You're welcome. There's no other way to get home, anyway, unless you wanted to take another dip in the creek."

No thanks. Once was more than enough.

"I suppose I could have walked the long way, that we're now driving."

"You wouldn't want to do that in the dark. At least until you're more used to the mountain. Cutting across the creek takes minutes but when you walk, it's an hour or so."

Used to the mountain? Yeah right. Like I'd be here long enough for that.

"When will the bridge be ready?"

He stole a glance at me. "Why? You planning on coming back over?"

I decided not to read too much into that.

"Um, sure. I want to learn how to gut fish like Theo. So I can be a real mountain girl."

Logan laughed out loud at that one. I didn't blame him. My big city street smarts were fairly useless on Deep Water Mountain, as I'd proved repeatedly.

"How long you planning on staying up here?" he asked as we pulled up to Bo's.

I started to answer, but as the truck turned the corner and its headlights swept across the front porch, I stopped.

The front door was open.

Like wide open.

13

AVA STONE

I FROZE, MY HAND ON THE DOOR HANDLE. I DIDN'T KNOW whether to cower in the truck or run inside and defend my property.

If I were at home, I'd call the cops.

But here? I had no fucking idea what to do. Did they even have cops?

Or was this the kind of place where people took the law into their own hands? I had a feeling I knew the answer.

"Ava, did you leave your front door open?"

It took a second to find my voice. "Um. No," I squeaked.

Logan looked around the yard, but in the dark, I don't know what he was looking for. Then, he reached behind his seat, returned with a large tire iron, and grabbed a flashlight out of the glove box.

"C'mon. Stay behind me."

Holyshitholyshitholyshit.

Thank god he'd brought me home. What the hell would I have done if I'd arrived alone?

I *knew* the woods weren't safe. I didn't care what people said. Logan and his buds could scoff all they wanted. But danger lurked everywhere, like I'd known, and now I was coming face to face with it.

Logan left the engine running with the lights shining on the front of the house and started walking toward it, holding the tire iron. He peeked over his shoulder and gestured for me to catch up, which I did.

I was so terrified he was lucky I didn't jump right up his ass.

"Watch your step," he whispered, pointing at the busted-through front stair.

Like I could forget that was there.

When we got to the door, he shone the light into the house, sweeping it across the kitchen and living room.

Nothing.

"Let's check the bedrooms."

I followed him so closely I could smell the detergent he used on his clothes. I was dying to grab his hand for reassurance, but I barely knew him and besides, I didn't want to look any more chicken shit than I already was.

Logan pushed open the door to my bedroom, scanning it with his light. I watched him look in the closet and under the bed.

"Nothing here." He looked in the other room, which didn't have much in it except for an old twin bed and dresser.

He walked over to the front of the house and flicked on the lights.

"Do you think it was a burglar?" I asked.

He surveyed the room. "It seems highly unlikely. There's really nothing here to take. Do you see anything missing?"

I looked around. "The only thing I have of value is that laptop right there," I said, pointing.

He nodded, then walked over to the door and started jiggling the knob.

After a minute, he looked at me. "I think I may have found the culprit."

"What?" I asked, still skeeved out that someone might have been in Bo's house. Well, *my* house.

"Come. I'll show you."

"What is it?" I asked.

"See this latch here?" he asked, pushing it in and out.

"Yeah?"

"It was stuck. It didn't extend, and therefore couldn't hold the door shut."

I looked up at him, realizing how tall he was. And he smelled so damn good... like the woods or something.

Hold it. I didn't like the woods. They were scary and they definitely didn't smell good.

"So... um..." I was having trouble with my words. "You don't think it was a person?"

He shook his head. "No. But this door needs to be fixed. You don't want any animals coming in."

No kidding, buddy.

"Okay," I breathed.

"But relax. Humans are much more dangerous than animals."

I wasn't so sure about that.

Then, he stepped back, putting some distance between us.

Darn.

He looked around the house. "Yup. Just how I remember it. Bo was nothing if not a creature of habit."

I took a breath, not realizing I was holding mine. "Hey, would you like a glass of wine? You know, in thanks for driving me home?"

"Oh. Sure. Okay." He made his way over to Bo's ratty old sofa.

I ran to the kitchen to grab the nice bottle of red I'd brought with me and set it down on the coffee table.

"Would you like me to open it?" he offered.

"Sure."

He deftly used the wine key and the bottle was open in seconds.

Okay. He'd done that a few times before.

"Unfortunately, there are no wine glasses. But here are a couple jelly jars," I said, setting them down.

"That'll do." He sloshed the wine around in his glass, smelled it, and took a taste.

His eyes widened. "Holy shit. I haven't had wine like this in an age. You don't find stuff like this around here."

I sipped mine. It was heavenly, I had to agree.

"Did you drink wine often?" I asked. After interrogating the men earlier, I knew to scale back my nosiness.

He nodded, looking up at the cobwebs in the corners of the room.

"I used to run a company with my father. We were residential developers down valley."

"Really?"

"Yeah. But we had to declare bankruptcy after a bunch of lawsuits. So, I came up here."

"Sorry to hear about the company."

"Thank you. Anyway, I used to have a more boring, traditional life that included lots of good wine exactly like this." He laughed.

Wait a minute. Was he saying *I* had a boring, traditional life?

But before I could find out, he finished his wine and set his glass down. "Better get going. Early morning and all."

Which was when a brilliant idea popped into my head. "You know how to build stuff. Maybe you could help me with this cabin?"

I smiled as brightly as possible, remembering the pricey quote the contractor had laid on me.

He pressed his lips together and frowned.

"Oh, wait, Logan. I don't mean for free. I'd pay you. We'd settle on what needed to be done, and how much it would cost."

He started moving toward the door, but I was right

behind him. "Theo said you had Pete over. Didn't he give you a quote?"

I poured myself more wine. Logan might be done, but I was not. Not after the day I'd had. "Yes, he did. But it was more than I could afford. I'm on a… budget."

He looked around the house. Maybe he was considering it?

Or was he pretending to consider my suggestion out of obligation or politeness?

Maybe I shouldn't have asked him. I'd been presumptuous. "Don't worry about it. I shouldn't have put you on the spot."

I'd stepped into it once more. These guys were going to think I was a loser of epic proportions.

His gaze returned to mine, and I put a hand on the wall for balance, that's how intense his eyes were. "No. It's all right. How about I come back tomorrow and see the place in the daylight? What are your plans for it, anyway?"

Yes.

I felt the first surge of hope since the attorney had told me the place was mine.

"I figured I'd fix it up—nothing too drastic—and sell it. That will get me a little nest egg to buy a nice condo in the city."

He nodded slowly.

"You think I'm crazy?"

He shook his head. "No. Not at all. I used to want things like that, nice homes with all the fixings."

Hey. Was he back to insulting me? Even if it was unintentional…

"But, you know, my priorities changed."

I got the distinct feeling there was more to his story.

Should I ask?

But before I could, his eyes traveled down to my lips, where they stayed for a moment.

But only for a moment.

Because he kissed me.

14

LOGAN MEYER

What a fucking idiot.

Why did I go ahead and kiss Ava? She was *so* not my type, and besides, she'd soon be gone. Once she dumped the cabin, she'd never come back to Deep Water.

She hated the outdoors and wanted nothing to do with the mountains.

Not the woman for me, no doubt.

But sitting next to her at Bo's, drinking the best wine I'd tasted in years, did something to me.

It didn't hurt that she was fucking gorgeous, as silly as she looked in Theo's borrowed clothes. Her long dark hair and olive skin did something to me.

Some guys like blondes. Not me.

But even more stupid than kissing her, I'd agreed to

return the next morning to see how I could help with the house.

But that shit was like crack to me. I loved fixing up a rundown place. Taking something desperate for some TLC, bringing it back to life.

And Bo's place had potential. It had good bones and was on a nice piece of property.

Even if it were lacking a bathroom.

Which had always struck me as strange.

On my way back for the second day in a row, my truck bumped along Bo's rutted road, which he'd never wanted to fix. His reasoning was that if people came across it, they'd turn around and leave, either assuming the unmaintained road led nowhere, or that whatever was at the end of it wasn't worth the trouble. It wasn't that he didn't like people. He just didn't like *uninvited* people.

Right before I'd left the previous evening, when both Ava and I were both surprised by our kiss, she ran to a closet and returned with an armful of magazines.

Playboy magazines. Old *Playboy* magazines.

As if the night could get any weirder.

She thrust them at me. "I remembered Colton and Theo saying they liked these."

The issue on top was dated 1976, and the cover girl was painted in stars and stripes.

I accepted them because what else could I do? "They liked them when they were horny teenagers. But, thanks."

She was skeptical. "You don't think they like them now?"

Busted. Of course, they would. "I'll take them. Thank you. Well, thank you, *Bo*."

I planned to enjoy them too, not that I was about to admit it. I was always ready for some new jerking-off material.

And now, one day later, I was back at Bo's. Or should I say Ava's. At least the front door was closed this time. I'd rigged it until I could install a new mechanism.

I was already working on the house, wasn't I?

I knocked.

No answer.

I knocked again.

Footsteps thumped over the wooden floors. "Just a minute," a sleepy voice called.

The makeshift latch scraped against the old wood of the door, and when it flew open, Ava stood there in her nightgown.

A very thin, white nightgown.

I had not signed up for this, goddammit.

I fixed my gaze over her head and into the house.

"Hey, Logan. Good morning. C'mon in," she said, yawning and finger-combing her hair. "I was thinking about running out to get us bagels and coffee. What do you think?"

Okay. I had to laugh at that one.

"You can go for bagels, but you'll have to drive an hour each way to town."

Her face fell. "You're kidding. There are no stores nearby? I need food."

Jesus, I wish she'd put some clothes on. Her nipples

were dark and pointed, not something I needed to see when I was beating myself up for kissing her.

"There's a general store a couple miles away. But the closest thing they'll have to bagels is stale Wonderbread."

I must have been staring because she crossed her arms across her chest.

Down boy.

"I have yogurt and a couple energy bars. Would you like something?"

I just wanted to get to work. After kissing her the night before and seeing her in nightclothes just now, I was not, let us say, comfortable in my trousers.

"No. I'm good. I ate before I left. But if you want to go get some food, don't worry about me."

She nodded. "Okay. Do you know where you want to start?"

I looked out the front door onto the porch. "The stairs. That hole there is deadly. If you weren't careful some night, you could break a leg, not to mention cut yourself on rusty nails and shards of rotten wood."

I headed back to my truck to get my tools, hoping she would get dressed.

Jesus, what was I doing? She'd already met with Pete, who was one of the best contractors on the mountain. He could do this work, and I could stay home, looking at vintage Playboys and rubbing one out.

I didn't need to be tempted like this.

If she couldn't afford his fees, which I happened to know were always reasonable, was that my problem?

I sighed and got to work prying up the broken stair boards when Ava returned.

For fuck's sake, was she trying to mess with me?

She'd gotten dressed, but the change wasn't much of an improvement, evidenced by my twitching dick. In a pair of skin tight jeans and a plain white blouse, she was completely girl next door, yet fucking sexy at the same time.

I'd always been a sucker for a girl who didn't try too hard.

She propped herself up on the porch railing, resting on one butt cheek.

After a couple minutes, I looked up at her. "Ava, do you need something?"

Her face was calm, a far cry from the panic of the night before when she was certain deadly thugs had invaded her home. "I thought I might watch. See what I could learn."

All right. She was going to watch me fix the front steps. Nothing wrong with that. But if she asked me a shit load of dumb questions, I might have to send her back into the house.

"I'm surprised Bo lived with this level of disrepair," I said, measuring replacement boards.

"I know, right. What was he thinking? I mean, keeping the porch stairs in good shape doesn't seem like it would be too difficult for someone like him. Hell, he always could have hired you, ya know?"

She was right. It was a simple repair, nothing he had any reason to blow off. And yet, he did.

Ava swung her legs over the porch railing so she was right next to my head. "You never told me how much your work was going to cost, Logan."

I put one of the new stair boards in place before I looked up at her. "You told me your budget. I won't exceed that."

Okay. Now, I was being a dick. She'd told me she had five thousand dollars to spend. But the truth was, I didn't want her money. I wanted to help out old Bo, and as a result, help her too.

Before he'd passed, if I'd known Bo's front steps were falling apart, I would have fixed them for free, along with the rest of the house. How could I charge Ava for what I would have done for her uncle at no charge?

"Okay. Cool. But I can't imagine that would include adding a full bathroom to the house. Right?"

I knew she was going to hammer me about that.

Shit. I had a lot to do. But all I wanted to do was wrap my hand in that long hair of hers and give it a hard tug—

"Seriously, Logan. I can't possibly hope to sell this place without a real bathroom. Don't you agree?"

God, I wished she'd stop talking. Every time she moved her lips, all I wanted to do was press mine to them.

"Hey, you know what I could do? If it's super expensive to install a bathroom, I could pay you after the house sells. Or make you a part owner of the house, so you get your share after someone buys it."

I stood, my back aching from being bent for so long. Shit, it had been a while since I'd done work like this. "That's something to think about, Ava. I'll give it some thought. But the good news is that there is plumbing to the house. And that's half the battle with a bathroom."

She jumped off the railing, narrowly missing my saw. "Water?" she offered.

"Sure."

Bo, Bo, Bo. Did he leave this place to his niece, knowing our paths would eventually cross, so he could torment us three from the beyond?

It sure felt like it.

And honestly, while I wasn't going to say this to Ava, the house might be better off as a tear-down. Now that I was looking at it more closely, I wasn't sure it was salvageable. Her list of improvements was mainly cosmetic, but if the place had structural issues or termites, she was completely screwed. And I'd know the answer to that soon.

That is, unless some crusty old hunter wanted a cabin that made him feel like a frontier settler. In that case, the place would be perfect for him. But how many people were there like that?

"Here you go," Ava said, handing me a glass of water.

I looked at it skeptically. "Is that from the tap?"

She nodded. "Yeah, but I let it run until the rusty color went away."

Fucking Bo. It's a wonder he lived as long as he did.

I took a sip. It tasted okay, so I downed the glass. I figured it couldn't kill me.

Just then, Ava pulled her phone out of her pocket. "Oh. It's working. Shit. I hope I can find the good cell spot." She started hollering, "Hello? Hello?" while she ran around searching for a decent connection.

"Here I am," she sang, moving to the far end of the front porch. "How are you? And how's everything at the office?"

There were a lot of *uh-huhs* and *no kiddings*. And then the tall tales started.

"Oh yeah, I'm up here on Deep Water Mountain. My uncle's place? Oh, it's amazing. I'm getting a little work done on it, and then I'll sell. It's lovely up here. Really. You should see it."

I remembered back when I gave a shit about what people thought. When you're in that place, it wasn't hard to lie to impress them. Listening to Ava smooth talk her colleague—whoever it was—made me happy I was up on the mountain, rather than down in the rat race like I used to be, at the mercy of my father. Thank god that was no longer a part of my world.

The best thing I could do for Ava was help her fix up the place so she could sell it and say goodbye to the mountain. This was no place for a woman like her.

Even if she were stunning. And ballsy. And put her foot in her mouth on a regular basis.

But it didn't matter. She might be the kind of woman I could have dated in my prior life, but not now. I'd changed too much.

She reappeared and took her seat on the porch railing while I finished my repair.

"It was the office," she said, as if I didn't know that.

"Hope all is well there."

"Oh yeah. You know, I didn't want them to know the challenges I'm having with Bo's place. It's really none of their business."

Uh-huh. Whatever you say.

15

AVA STONE

"Wow. Logan, those look amazing."

I stepped back and admired the work he'd done on my front steps. Walking up and down them now was not a life-threatening endeavor.

"Thank you so much, Logan. I'm so excited."

"Happy to help," he said, his gaze focused on me rather than the house.

Was he going to kiss me again? Did he want to?

I was sure our kiss from the night before was simply a fluke, fueled by good wine and the dim lights of Bo's living room. But it had been so delicious—slow and sensual.

He'd put his hand under my chin and turned my head

towards him, and when our lips touched, he stroked the side of my cheek—

"I think I'm gonna tackle the doorknob next, and then move on to holes in the roof."

Right. He was here to fix up my house. Not kiss me.

Unfortunately.

"Excellent," I said, hoping these things didn't use up my five-thousand-dollar budget too fast. "Logan, how long do you think you need to complete all this?"

He tilted his head. "With or without the new bathroom?"

I wanted to say without the bathroom because that would be a big-ass undertaking, but the reality was, the cabin was worth next to nothing without it.

That's why I'd offered Logan part of the proceeds from the house's sale. I wasn't sure he was interested, though. And if he wasn't, I was screwed. My measly five thousand bucks would be eaten up in no time, long before we'd even started planning for the bathroom.

"*With* it, of course. I don't think the house will sell without one."

He took a deep breath. "Okay then. I'd say I could probably get it done in three weeks. Maybe less if the others feel like pitching in."

Shit. I couldn't hang out for that long. I supposed I could go back home and return on the weekends…

I had a damn job I needed to do.

Then I remembered the realtor was supposed to come over. He couldn't see the house like this.

I dug out the business card Bo's attorney had given

me. "Mr. Stinson? It's Ava Stone. Calling about my Uncle Bo's house."

Papers shuffled in the background. "Hello, Ava. I was about to head over your way."

That's what I was afraid of.

"Mr. Stinson, we're going to need to reschedule. The house needs more work than I'd thought."

I didn't mention the lack of plumbing facilities.

"Oh. I'm sorry to hear that. I was really looking forward to checking out the place. It's such a great location, near that old pond and creek."

Location might be all the place had going for it.

"I hope you called my contractor, Pete."

"Yes, he came over and gave me a quote. But he was out of my price range. I have a neighbor helping."

There was silence for a moment. "I don't know about that, Ava. Pete really is my go-to person for these things."

"When my house is done and you see all the work, maybe you'll have two go-to people."

I wrapped up the call, relieved that I'd caught him before he'd gotten here. If I wanted to get anything for the house, I had to make the best possible impression on him.

Speaking of which, the house had absolutely no 'curb appeal.' From the outside, it pretty much looked like a dump.

But a few flower boxes with bright red geraniums would give the place a huge boost. And I needed something to do while I was hanging out here.

Only problem was, I didn't know how to make flower boxes. But I did know how to use Google.

I stood at the end of the porch where I got the best cell reception and found instructions for making flower boxes. They didn't look too hard, and I was excited to try my hand at woodworking. I needed a new hobby anyway

"I'll be over at the shed, Logan. I need to gather the tools to make some flower boxes."

He looked up at me, unconvinced, then got back to what he was doing.

Uncle Bo, for all his eccentricities, actually had an awesome shed. I looked at the list of supplies I needed, thanks to Google, and got my hands on a screwdriver and screws, and small nails and a hammer. I grabbed some scraps of wood that looked about the right size, but I didn't see a drill.

Crap.

Fortunately, there were a couple giant tool boxes. I set down what I had gathered so far and lifted the lid on the first box. It contained rusty old saws and other unidentifiable items, so I moved on to the next.

But as soon as I lifted the lid, I found a big snake curling itself around the box's contents.

It caught me by such surprise that I shrieked, dropped the lid, and left the shed so fast I tripped and ended up on the ground on my ass.

Seconds later, Logan came running.

"What's wrong? What happened Ava?" he asked, frowning.

I had a major case of the heebie-jeebies. I wasn't sure I could even go back inside the shed.

I pointed with a shaking finger. "S... s... snake!"

"Oh. That's all? I thought maybe you'd cut your hand off or something."

Sorry to disappoint.

"Where was it?"

I pointed.

He slowly lifted the lid. "Oh. That's nothing but a garden snake."

To my horror, he picked up the snake right behind its head, and stepped out of the shed. Walking around the side, he chucked it into the woods.

"There you go. All safe and sound now."

He headed back to the house, his tool belt hanging low on his hips, and while he was walking, stripped off his shirt and wiped his face and head with it.

Jesus, he was gorgeous.

And right before he turned the corner to enter the house, he turned around and caught me staring.

SHAKEN BY THE SNAKE SIGHTING, I piled my window-box materials into a pile, and decided to take a break.

"Hey, Logan," I said as he started climbing a ladder to the roof. "You're making good progress."

Maybe he could start the bathroom… tomorrow?

He stopped climbing and took a deep breath. Then he came back down and faced me with crossed arms.

"I am making good progress Ava. Or at least I was."

What a grump.

"Anyway, can you tell me how to get to the general store?"

"Sure. It's a few miles *that* way," he said pointing.

"Oh. So the direction opposite from where I drove in from?"

He raised his eyebrows and sighed.

What a jerk. He'd better not think he was going to kiss me again or he'd be getting a nice smack across the face.

"Do you need anything?" I asked.

"Sure. How about a bottle of water?"

Guess he didn't like my tap water. Couldn't blame him.

A LOUD BELL jingled when I pulled open the door to the Deep Water Mountain Store. Walking inside, I understood what Logan had meant about white bread. The place had the basics in addition to a lot of junk food and alcohol, and not a whole lot more.

It reminded me of a 7-11, but maybe a smidgeon nicer with its small produce section.

I wandered around the store filling up a basket when I got an idea. I threw flour, sugar, and yeast in my basket.

I was going to learn to make bread, and show Logan that I wasn't completely useless.

"Will this be all?" the clerk asked, a slight, pretty woman in a flannel shirt.

"I think I'm set. I'm going to try and make bread."

She looked impressed. "You ever done it before?"

I shook my head. "No. You?"

She shrugged. "My mother used to. But not me. Say, where are you staying?"

"At my uncle's cabin. He passed away and left it to me."

Surprise crossed her face. "Really? Who was your uncle?"

"Bo Devine. Did you know him?"

The woman's face got pale and her jaw went slack.

She finished ringing up my purchases and hurriedly stuffed them into a bag.

"I'm Ava," I said, extending my hand.

"I'm Ruthie." She sniffled, and I realized her eyes were full of tears.

"I guess you were friends with him? I'm sorry you didn't know."

She shrugged resignedly. "Well. I hadn't seen him in a while. But I liked him."

Seemed like everyone liked Bo.

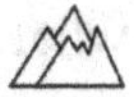

16

THEO PAYNE

"I HEARD A SCREAM EARLIER TODAY, AVA. WHAT WAS that?"

She looked up from where she was sitting on the ground amid a pile of tools and several unevenly cut pieces of wood, one of which she was furiously sanding.

Was she trying to *make* something? Out of wood? By hand?

She stopped sanding and tried to hide the chewed up pieces of wood by gathering them into a small stack. "Oh, hi, Theo. It was nothing."

Her face slowly turned a shade of bright red.

Logan came around the corner, his tool belt swinging heavily. "Oh. Hey, Theo. I thought I heard your voice. How's the bridge coming?"

I looked between he and Ava. Were they avoiding each other?

"It's good. Will probably be done today. Say, I heard a scream earlier. Did something happen? Is everyone okay?"

Logan laughed. "Oh that. Ava was in Bo's shed and saw a little snake."

Glaring at Logan, she got to her feet. Now that she wasn't wearing Bo's clothes, or mine, I had to say she looked damn good in her blue jeans and blouse.

Unfortunately, she was covered in dust from sitting on the ground, as well as chips of wood from whatever she was trying to make.

She brushed herself off. "It wasn't *little*, and it scared the hell out of me." She scowled again in his direction.

I looked at Logan, who was trying not to smile. "It was a garden snake, Ava. They are not huge. Anyway, Theo, I threw it in the woods."

Ava looked at the woods uncomfortably, then back at the shed. "You don't think there are a lot of snakes around here, do you?"

She was surrounded by freaking forest. What did she think lived in there?

"Of course—" Logan started to say.

But I cut him off. "Don't worry, Ava. There are only a few and they're very shy. They do their best to stay out of your way." No reason to scare the shit out of her. She wouldn't be on the mountain for long and it wasn't likely she'd see another snake.

She wrinkled her nose and shuddered.

"What is this you're making, Ava?"

"I am making window boxes for the front of the house. I found the instructions on Google. They looked pretty easy. But my pieces aren't matching up," she said, gesturing at the mess on the ground. "I don't know why. I measured each piece multiple times."

I bent to pick up the piece of wood she'd been sanding and ran my finger over the crooked end. "When you first start working with wood, it's hard to get everything to perfectly match up. Maybe I can help you with this later."

She brightened. "Really? You think so? That would be so cool. I want the house to have a little curb appeal before the realtor comes over."

I wasn't entirely sure what curb appeal was, but it was going to take a lot more than flower boxes to give Bo's house any sort of appeal.

"Anyway, I made bread. Yeah. Can you believe it?"

Wow. She was becoming a regular Annie Oakley.

"Want to try some? Wait, I'll go get it."

While she was gone, I turned to Logan. "She made bread? Seriously?"

"I heard her banging around in the kitchen while I was up on the roof. I knew I smelled something. I thought it was toast."

I watched her come flying out the front door of Bo's house with a big smile on her face.

"She sure is pretty, isn't she?"

Logan shrugged.

Fucker. I knew he liked her too. Couldn't fool me.

"Okay. Here is a slice for each of you. Let me know what you think."

She held out a small plate with thick slices of home-made white bread. It looked good and smelled even better.

Ava might be out of her element, but she sure knew how to adapt.

I raised my slice like it was a beer. "Hats off to the chef—"

But I was interrupted by choking sounds. I watched Logan's eyes water and his face turn red. I slapped him on the back a couple times as he caught his breath. Dude needed to slow down when he ate.

I dug into my own slice and immediately realized what was wrong with Logan because the same thing happened to me. I turned away and coughed until my throat was clear again. I wiped my eyes and turned back to Ava.

Her smile gone, concern washed over her face. "You okay? Swallow wrong?"

Was she fucking kidding? That bread must have been about the worst, driest thing I'd ever put in my mouth.

A bite of sand from the Sahara Desert would have been more appetizing.

I nodded, catching my breath. "Yeah. Just need to slow down a bit."

Her smile returned and she bounced up and down. "I can't believe I made this. It's my first time!" She took a slab and stuffed it into her mouth, closing her eyes and moaning while she consumed it in glee.

Somehow, she managed not to choke on it.

Logan and I looked at each other, happy to be alive.

17

THEO PAYNE

"Hey, question for you two."

Ava extended her plate of bread, offering us more.

I rubbed my stomach, indicating I was full. I didn't know how Logan turned her down and I didn't care. He was on his own.

"What's that, Ava?" he asked.

She put a hand on her hip while nibbling the last slice of her deadly bread. "When I went to the general store earlier, I met a woman named Ruthie."

I stole a glance at Logan.

"I told her about Bo's passing, and she really got upset."

Sounded about right.

"Ruthie was one of Bo's… good friends. If you know what I mean."

At first, Ava's face was blank but then understanding washed over her face.

"Ohhhh…" she said, trying not to laugh.

I didn't want to say booty call. Doubted Bo wanted his niece to know that much about his private life. On the other hand, Ava was no idiot. She could figure stuff out.

"I was sorry to see her get upset. But I'm glad she knows now."

While she was chatting, Ava kept fidgeting. I finally figured out why and it wasn't because she was so excited about her bread.

"Hey, did you want to use the bathroom over at our house, Ava?"

Her eyes widened. "Oh. Do you think I could? You know, I hate that outhouse so I just started peeing by the side of the house. But with you guys around, I've been… holding it."

Okay… TMI. But I was glad to help the lovely lady out.

"Why don't you go ahead and drop that plate back in the house and we'll go?"

She skipped off as Logan and I watched her very tight jeans on her very cute butt.

"What the fuck was up with that bread, bro?" Logan said, taking a swig from the water bottle attached to his tool belt.

"I know right. I give her props for trying but she's got a way to go with her baking skills."

As I said that, she came bounding back out. "I can't wait to see the bridge. Is it solid enough to walk over?"

"Yeah. I need to do a little more work on the railing. Do you think you can make it over without falling in?"

She put her hands on her hips and smirked. "If I do fall in, I know you have clothes I can borrow, Theo."

"If you're going to make a habit of wearing my clothes, I may have to buy some for you to keep at my house."

Any reason to get her over to our house... and to take off her clothes. Preferably with my help.

"Hey, Logan, keep up the good work," I said, waving back over my shoulder as I hit the path to the bridge with Ava on my trail.

"Yeah. Thanks bud," he called after us.

With her sneakers on, Ava was dressed better than the first time I'd seen her in the woods, when she was spying on me and nearly wiped out trying to run back up the embankment to her house.

As we crossed the new bridge with the incomplete railing, I took her hand to help her, and when we reached the other side, I didn't let go.

She didn't seem to mind.

"Okay. You know where the bathroom is," I said when we got to the house.

When she returned, she helped herself to a seat at our kitchen counter. She might not be much of a mountain girl, but she did carry a certain amount of confidence that I admired. She wasn't afraid of much.

Aside from snakes.

"It's so nice of you to help someone you barely know. I want to thank you for being so kind. This has been the best part of inheriting Bo's house. Meeting all of you."

I'd have to agree. I was sorry Bo had passed but thrilled he'd brought his niece to us.

Maybe that had been his plan…?

I took a seat at the counter next to Ava. "I think you should stay longer. I know you're supposed to leave in a couple days but that's not enough to finish what you need to do, and also really appreciate the magic of the mountain."

Biting her bottom lip, she looked at her hands. "You know. I've kind of been thinking the same. I'm having fun, in spite of some of the hardships."

"Do you like living where you do? In the city? I've only ever lived up here on the mountain. I sometimes wonder what I'm missing," I said.

"That's so funny. I was thinking I've only ever really been a city person. I've never lived surrounded by nature. Snakes notwithstanding, it's pretty cool." She laughed. "And I do like living in the city. I mean, it's all I really know. But don't beat yourself up for making a life up here. You know how many people would love your life?"

I realized that while we were talking, Ava and I had moved closer and closer together. Finally, I had no choice but to kiss her.

And so I did.

18

AVA STONE

I'D KISSED LOGAN JUST THE DAY BEFORE.

And now I was kissing Theo.

What were these mountain men going to think of their city girl neighbor?

Nothing horrible, hopefully. It seemed Uncle Bo was a bit of a horn dog, so maybe it was fine for me to be one, too.

Seriously. It was only fair. Why should guys have all the fun?

What were the girls at home going to think when I told them?

Actually, I already knew. As soon as they found out there were hotties up here, they'd be lining up to be weekend guests at Uncle Bo's, at least until I sold the place.

I'd tell them there was no indoor plumbing.

They wouldn't care.

And that the only way to bathe was at the kitchen sink with a sponge.

They still wouldn't care.

That they might have to leave at home their designer boots and cashmere sweaters.

They… might actually care about that.

Hey, every girl dreams of a hot, strong, protective outdoorsman, right? And that dream wasn't going down easy, I could say that with confidence.

It was silly to worry. I was out of here in a few days, anyway. Even if Theo did suggest I stick around…

Which was becoming more likely, the longer he ran kisses up the side of my neck right there in his kitchen.

He was so different from the men at home with their manufactured scents and perfectly coiffed hair. Instead of chemicals, Theo smelled of pine and the forest, and slightly like a man who'd done a hard day's work. His long dirty blond hair was pulled into a messy ponytail, and his face was scruffy from a couple days of not shaving.

But what was most mesmerizing was the way he looked at me between kisses, making each one more intimate than the last.

It was almost too much, and I wanted to close my eyes to create some distance.

But I didn't.

I let his gaze drill mine, like he was invading me and

my thoughts. It was intimidating, but I was willing to give him a chance at really seeing me—something I rarely did with a guy.

He ran kisses along my temples and over my ears. "I love your hair," he murmured, running his fingers through it and taking large handfuls.

It had been so long since anyone had touched my hair, I'd forgotten how heavenly it was to be stroked that way.

Finally, after teasing me for what seemed ages, he brought his lips to mine, softly at first, brushing back and forth, and then urgently taking the kiss he wanted. I kept my eyes open until his fell closed and mine followed suit, the dark letting me fall deeper into him.

He took me by the hand and led me to the sofa. He laid me back, holding my arms above my head and trailed kisses along my neck until he reached the open neckline of my white blouse. His gaze on mine, he opened two buttons until my lacy bra was exposed, and kissed my breasts.

Goodness. I didn't think I'd ever been kissed by someone who'd taken his time like Theo was. And it made sense.

Why hurry? Where did we have to be? No one was waiting on us and we were waiting on no one.

Time was like that in the mountains, I was learning. Schedules had different meanings than they did back at home.

Where my job was waiting for me.

I'd called my boss earlier that day, apologizing profusely for having been gone.

"Ava, you've been away from the office for the two days that bookended the weekend. We'll survive without you. In fact, you have so much vacation time you've never used, it's about time you took advantage of it," she'd said.

I supposed she was right. And of course, they'd get by just fine without me for a few days.

But I didn't want them to. I wanted them to need me, if I were honest with myself. My job made me feel important. I got shit done there. I showed results. I was competent.

Unlike up in the mountains, where I couldn't make a freaking flower window box, and the bread I'd baked tasted like shit.

Even if Logan and Theo claimed to like it. They were only being polite. I knew that.

Theo pulled back from kissing me and stared.

Oh my god, the way he looked at me was so freaking hot.

"Hey, Theo, this is the part where you should offer me a glass of wine." I laughed.

A smile slowly spread across his face. "I can do you one better than that. Wait right here."

19

AVA STONE

He walked to the kitchen, returning with two small glasses and a mason jar full of some clear liquid. "This is my grandmother's moonshine recipe," he said, handing me a glass.

No way.

He poured us each some, clinked my glass, and took a healthy swig.

From my spot on the couch, I watched, afraid to follow suit.

He gestured with his chin. "Go ahead. Try a sip. It's kind of like whiskey."

"But it's clear. Isn't whiskey supposed to be brownish?"

He nodded. "Commercially produced whiskey is, for

sure, because it's been aged. But when whiskey comes out of the still, this is what it looks like."

"That's wild. And your grandparents used to make this?" I took a whiff. It wasn't too bad.

"Yup. Although, over the years my father and then my brother and I improved the recipe. It's not nearly as crude as what my grandmother made. C'mon now. Are you gonna try it?"

Might as well give it a shot. I was doing all sorts of other things for the first time.

I let a teeny bit pass my lips, and when it didn't burn my mouth raw, I took a more substantial sip. But not a swig like Theo had.

I grimaced anyway. I couldn't help it. I was more of a wine girl.

Theo laughed and took my glass. "Yeah, it's an acquired taste. What did ya think?"

My throat was burning, but it wasn't too bad. "It's strange. It tastes like corn."

"Yeah. That's what it's made of."

"And you like it? Like you could drink it every night?"

He shook his head. "Oh hell no. We bust it out for special occasions. I could never drink this every day."

Just then, there was a screech from outside the house, like a dog that might have rabies.

"Oh my god," I said, bolting up straight, my heart pounding. "What the hell was that?"

I heard it again, but this time it lasted longer. "Did you hear that?" I hissed.

Exactly when I was thinking the mountains weren't all that bad, some dangerous creature ruined it for me.

Theo took my hand. "It's a coyote. Is this the first one you've heard since you've been here? They're all over the place. He's looking for his pack."

Great. Just great. Coyotes all over. And these guys didn't think the woods were dangerous?

Theo must have read my thoughts. "Ava, coyotes won't bother you. Humans are way too big for them to mess with. I don't know if you realize this, but your life in the city is much more dangerous than it is here on Deep Water Mountain."

The city is more dangerous than the mountains? Was he crazy?

But he had a point. I knew way more people who'd been mugged than had been attacked by coyotes. Or bitten by snakes.

So there was that.

"I feel safe here," I said, relaxing back onto the sofa and hoping Theo would return to kissing me.

I hadn't been with a guy in so long. There'd been one who'd pursued me hard, but the minute I'd slept with him, he'd ghosted me.

Fucker.

He *tried* to ghost me, I should say. Problem was, we worked together.

But I held my head up and did a bang-up job of ignoring him. I also got my hair done and bought some sexy new clothes to torment him.

Had he noticed?

Probably not.

But I felt better.

And now here I was with Theo.

"Hey, Theo, what's up with your brother and Logan? They're not nearly as nice as you."

He laughed. "Oh, they're plenty nice. They just take longer to warm up. They're… more reserved."

Yeah. No shit.

"But I don't want to talk about them right now," he said, leaning closer.

I held up a finger. "I have something to tell you."

His eyebrows rose. "Okay. What?"

"I kissed Logan the other day."

Another smile slid across his face. "Okay. Cool."

Cool? Like, he was okay with that?

These mountain men were weird.

But if he was okay with it, I sure as hell was.

Wrapping my arms around his neck, I pulled him to me, this time wanting him to do more than just open my blouse a couple buttons.

We were clearly on the same page. He lay above me on the sofa, supporting himself with one arm, our legs intertwined. When I pressed against him I found he had a huge hard-on, and when he pressed back, he groaned.

Hell, yeah.

I opened his flannel shirt and pushed it off his shoulders, running my hands over his warm, tan skin. His muscles rippled as he moved, and I marveled over their perfect definition. I guess felling trees and building bridges and whatever shit mountain men did really kept a person in shape.

"You're beautiful, you know that?" he murmured.

I pulled him to me again, desperate for his lips. I wanted him to take me away from the snakes and coyotes, and to be honest, everything about Uncle Bo's mess of a cabin. I didn't know what the hell would come of that wreck of a home, but at that moment, it didn't matter. I was floating and it was fucking amazing.

Theo's lips left mine and he opened my blouse the rest of the way, pushing my bra up. He inhaled sharply when he saw my naked breasts, and pushed them together so he could easily kiss one after the other.

When my nipples were wet, he rolled them between his fingers.

It felt so good that I arched into him, and when I did, he closed them tighter. A flood of sensation exploded in my core and shot through to my extremities. I gasped and dropped my head back on the sofa.

He released my breasts and moved down to my jeans, which he opened and shimmied below my hips. He was kissing his way down my belly when there was a sound at the front door.

We both looked up in time to see his brother, Colton, come flying in and slam a huge, dead turkey on the kitchen table.

20

COLTON PAYNE

FUCK IF MY BROTHER WASN'T MAKING OUT ON THE SOFA with our hot neighbor, Ava. Actually, they were doing a lot more than making out, because he had her pants pulled down and her tits hanging out.

She made an effort to cover her privates by turning toward the sofa, which resulted in showing her lovely backside. Theo just smiled.

I stood at the edge of the living room, looking at them and shaking my head. "Got a turkey."

My brother nodded. "I can see that, Bro."

Ava, who'd turned to look over her shoulder and acknowledge my bird, smiled and nodded, too, as if she were happy for me.

"I'm going back outside to clean up."

I left them there. Would they retire to a bedroom, pack it in, or keep going as they were? I wished I had someone to make a bet with.

If I knew my brother, which of course I did, I'd say he would be perfectly content to keep at it on the living room sofa without a care for who might see.

If Ava were the sort of woman I thought, she was probably dying of embarrassment at that very moment, indignantly pushing Theo off her, jumping to her feet to get dressed, and berating him for not knowing someone could walk through the door at any moment.

Yeah, I knew her type. I'd almost married someone a lot like her.

Before I was shipped out to the Middle East, back in my Army days, I'd said goodbye to my fiancé for a year-long deployment. While we kept in touch, taking full advantage of modern technology with Skype and such, I came home to find out she'd had another guy keep our bed warm in my absence.

To say I was devastated was an understatement. I packed a duffel of clothes and headed up to Deep Water, to my family place, which was occupied by my brother. Never saw the woman again. Never saw any of the stuff I'd left behind, either, but that didn't matter. It had probably been used by the douchebag who was boning her, anyway.

I turned the outdoor faucet on full blast and braced myself for the cold water. I was pretty pleased with that afternoon's hunting expedition. It wasn't hard to shoot a turkey, per se, but they were hard to come by on the mountain, and when I did see one, I was pretty psyched.

I loved turkey, and when I did get one, we usually set ourselves up for a feast. Other times, when we didn't have time for all that, we'd butcher the bird and freeze it so we could take out the parts we wanted a few at a time.

But, because today's catch had given me a run for my money, I was filthy. I kicked my boots and socks off and stripped off my clothes. I splashed enough water on myself to get the dirt and blood off, then rinsed my clothes and hung them over the porch railing before returning to the house. I was fucking freezing, but I stuck my head under the stream to get the rest of the grime off. I could take a real shower, with warm water, afterward.

When I walked into the house, I was surprised to see Theo and Ava still going at it on the sofa. I stopped at the edge of the living room and looked at them.

Ava attempted to cover herself again, and Theo rolled his eyes at me. "Hey, asshole, why don't you put some clothes on?"

I looked down at myself, naked as the day I was born. "What? You two are right in the middle of the living room mostly undressed. Why can't I walk through my own house naked if I want?"

Yeah, I wanted Ava to get a good look.

And she sure as hell did. For a moment, I think she forgot she was on the sofa with Theo. Poor bastard.

"Fine," I said, heading for the bathroom, where I wrapped a white towel around my waist.

I returned to the kitchen and threw the turkey in the

sink while I covered the table with paper before I started the fun job of plucking the dead bird.

"Thanks for the towel, Colton," Ava teased from the sofa.

"You're welcome. We're not modest around here, Ava. Shit, you can walk around naked if you want to, too."

She giggled. "Maybe I will."

"Look at you all. Diving into the moonshine." I grabbed myself a glass from the cupboard and headed to the living room to join them. The turkey could wait.

Theo positioned himself to give Ava privacy while I helped myself to a drink and took a seat, towel and all.

Was I a dick for cockblocking my brother that way? Maybe. But he'd be fine.

"What do you think of the moonshine, Ava? It's our family recipe."

She peeked around from behind Theo. "It took a few sips to get used to, but I kind of like it. Even though it's super strong."

I held my glass up to her as if we were toasting. "You're right. You gotta be careful with this stuff. It'll knock you on your ass before you know what hit you."

Theo got a naughty grin on his face. "Hey, Colt, Ava here was just telling me she wanted to kiss you. She's already kissed Logan and me."

She slapped his arm. "I did *not* say that, you jerk," she squealed.

He laughed. "Okay. Maybe you didn't. But I know you want to."

My brother was hooking me up.

I tapped the arm of my chair. "Theo, I think it's up to the lady."

Theo and I looked at her.

"Ava, stop hiding behind my brother. You know you're a beautiful woman. Why don't you let me see you?"

She tilted her head as she considered my words. As she was always saying, she was a *city girl*. She'd probably done some wild shit in her day. But I'd bet money she'd not played with two brothers. Or any mountain men for that matter.

"Okay," she said boldly, crawling out from behind Theo. She pushed herself up on the sofa and swung her legs around.

Damn. I'd have to thank my brother later. This was one beautiful woman.

She sat on the sofa facing me, her posture defiant and sexy as hell. All she was wearing was an unbuttoned white blouse and bra underneath it.

Her olive skin was smooth and taut. I imagined it was soft, and if all went according to plan, I'd have the chance to find out for myself. My gaze traveled from hers, down past the lacy bra holding her nice round tits, to her flat stomach.

"Open your legs," I demanded.

She blinked her eyes slowly and shifted on the sofa, parting her legs a couple inches.

Yes, I was going to like this very much.

"More."

Her breath caught, which she tried to hide by pressing her lips together. But her efforts were not lost on either my brother, or me. She spread her legs wider, this time giving me a perfect look at her smooth, shaved pussy.

There was no doubt I'd been in the mountains too goddamn long. I knew from porn that shaved pussies were all the rage, but it didn't seem to have caught on with the few mountain girls I messed around with from time to time.

So yeah, it had been a while since I'd seen a bare pussy, and it was so goddamn pretty my cocked popped a hard-on so big it hurt. It also knocked off the white towel I was wearing around my waist.

"Now, take off that shirt and bra."

She glanced at Theo, who nodded at her. Sliding the blouse off her shoulders, she tossed it to the floor, then reached behind her back to unhook the bra, which followed.

There our lovely new neighbor sat, naked and delicious, and all I could think was how badly I wanted to taste her.

"Hey, Brother," I said to Theo, "you mind if I lick this girl's pussy?"

Ava's lips parted slightly, and her eyelids grew heavy.

Yeah, I had her right where I wanted her.

I stood, the towel falling completely to the floor, and walked over to the sofa where she sat next to Theo. I got to my knees before her and pushed her legs apart. There, before me, was a glistening pink pussy, and as I moved closer, I could smell her excitement. My hard dick bounced against my stomach, and I had to take a deep breath to avoid coming right there.

"She looks nice, doesn't she, Theo?"

"Fuck yeah," he breathed, leaning her back on the sofa and kissing her while he played with her tits.

Ava was fumbling with Theo's blue jeans, which for some reason he was still wearing. I knew she wanted to get at his cock, but that wasn't my goddamn problem.

With one hand stroking my own dick, I used the other to gently part Ava's pussy lips. Her insides were a delicate shell pink, and when I ran my tongue through them, she tasted like the ocean—clean and salty and fresh.

But it was when she moaned that I really nearly lost it.

Her sounds were hungry and pleading—as if I were to stop, she might lose her mind. She bucked her hips as if demanding more, and I was only too happy to oblige.

Theo, in the meantime, had finally gotten his jeans off, and Ava was handling his dick like a pro. He pumped himself into her hand while their lips brushed each other's and he pulled at her nipples.

I slipped a finger into her wet opening, and she moaned again, louder this time. I glanced at Theo, who smiled at her reaction and nodded at me.

I added a second finger to her pretty pussy, and ran my tongue over her clit. With her free hand, she began to pound the sofa and gasp for air, so I increased my suction and the speed I fucked her with my fingers.

It was when her thighs began to quake that I knew I had her. Theo growled and spurted all over her tits and while she ran the fingers of her free hand through his cum, she bucked against my mouth one last time and screamed, convulsing around my fingers and coming in my face. Her juices flowed, and I took them as fast as they came, relishing every drop. My own explosion came a moment later. I directed my cock at her stomach, where I emptied the biggest load of cum I'd ever shot.

With Theo's dick still in her hand, she looked up at us and smiled that sweet, sexy grin that had got me on the first night she'd come over, when she was wet and dirty and had fucked up my hunting.

21

AVA STONE

"WHAT HAVE WE HERE?"

Holyfuckingshit.

It was Logan. Looking down on Colton, Theo, and me. In bed.

I felt like I'd been caught by my parents with a boy in my bedroom.

"Hey, Logan. What's up?" Colton asked, his tired cock falling on his leg.

Rolling over on his side, Theo propped his head up on his hand. "Logan. Why don't you join us?"

What?

Shouldn't he have checked with me first? I mean, it wasn't just *any* kind of party we were having. This one was special.

And sexy.

And now that I thought about it, Logan would be the perfect addition.

After Colton and Theo had worked me over so hard that I was barely conscious, they carried me to their guest room where there was a giant king-sized bed. I lay between the two of them—I was pretty sure I'd died and gone to heaven—and we talked, laughed, and stole the occasional kiss. Or in Colton's case, copped a feel or two.

And now that I lay there like I was freaking Roman goddess flanked by her servants, Logan's gaze wandered the length of my body as if he were memorizing every inch he could get his eyes on.

And his gaze, as it traveled, left a trail of burning heat on my skin, so hot my breath came harder like there was less oxygen in the room. I moved my hair in front of one of my shoulders to cool my neck, where a light mist had begun to develop.

Had Uncle Bo known I'd take to these guys the way I had? How could he? I'd had no contact with him since I was a kid. And yet something about my lying there on the bed with Colton and Theo, and Logan soon to join us, felt so predestined, like it was supposed to happen.

Wait a minute. I'd clearly been reading too many romance novels.

Jesus, girl.

When Logan was done looking me over, his gaze settled on mine and he ran a hand over his bald head. His Adam's apple bobbed as he swallowed, the only movement showing he was affected by what was in front of him. Without a word, he slipped his jacket off, kicked his boots aside, and unbuttoned his flannel shirt.

And damn if he didn't have a physique that the angels would sing for with his taut belly and hard pecs.

He finally broke the silence. "Theo. Gimme some of that moonshine," he said, gesturing to the nightstand where we'd left the mason jar and our glasses.

Colton cupped one of my breasts. "Ava, do we have room for another?

Logan took a swig of the moonshine Theo handed him and set the glass back down.

"I don't know. I haven't been invited by our lovely lady yet."

I untangled myself from Colton and scooted over to the edge of the bed, where I sat, my legs parted wide enough to pull Logan between them. I began to open his belt and stared up at him. "Is this enough of an invitation?"

A smile spread across his face, and he buried his fingers in my hair. "I suppose so."

I worked the front of his pants until they were open and slipped them and his boxers down below his thighs.

I ran my hands over his hard ass cheeks while I watched his erection bob in the space between us. It swayed heavily, hitting his belly button then brushing the side of my cheek as I brought my face closer to it.

His hands on my head, he maneuvered his hips in the direction of my mouth, which I let hang open like a hungry little animal waiting for its feeding. With a hand around the base of his cock, I stroked him to his tip and brought it to my lips, finally tasting his precum.

I closed my lips around his cockhead, and he groaned with the pain and pleasure of knowing satisfaction lay just around the corner. Behind me, Theo rubbed his cock on my back while playing with my tits, and Colton sat back watching the two guys sandwich me.

I'd never had a threesome, never mind a foursome, but so far I would say I highly recommend it.

Three sexy, strong mountain men were working me over, and I was nearly catatonic with pleasure.

Uncle Bo's cabin might have been a disappointment, but his neighbors sure weren't. This was one weekend away I'd never forget.

Maybe I'd write it up for *Cosmo*. Why not?

Logan's cock banged into the back of my throat, and with my hands on his ass, I pulled him to me harder. I wanted more of him, as much as I could possibly take, and to give him pleasure like nothing he'd ever experienced. With him deep in my mouth, I leaned back to look up at him and found him gazing down at me, wearing a small smile of approval or appreciation, or something like that. I couldn't be sure, and it didn't matter.

With Logan in front of me and Theo behind, Colton was to my left, stroking himself faster and faster, his orgasm close. With a growl, he released his load on my tits. His cum was warm and thick, and just as I started to run my fingers through it, Theo appeared on my right and did the same. I was so turned on I sucked Logan even faster. He grabbed fistfuls of my hair one last time and thrust his cock in my mouth, spurting faster than I could swallow. The overflow ran down my chin to my chest, mixing with the other guys' cum.

They laid me back on the bed while we all caught our breath. Theo arrived with a warm, wet towel and began to wipe me clean. Logan smoothed the hair out of my face and kissed my temple while Colton kissed my neck.

"You're very pretty, Ava," he said. "If I'd known Bo had a niece like you, I would have dragged him down the mountain to introduce us."

I looked around. "All of you?"

They laughed and nodded.

"Of course," Theo said. "Or would you rather choose from among the three of us?"

Was he kidding? What woman would limit herself when she could have all three of these men?

AVA STONE

LOGAN GAVE ME HIS ROBE, AND I WANDERED AROUND THE house in it while Colton made us a delicious stew, with a vegetarian version for his brother.

"Where are these vases from? They're so unique."

Their crowded bookcases were interspersed with the most beautiful pottery I'd ever seen. It was brilliantly colored with swirls and stars and rosettes, all perfectly geometric and in harmony.

Colton looked up from his stirring. "I got all that when I was in the Middle East with the Army. They had these vendors come on base once a week and some of them had these amazing Islamic handicrafts. I would have bought more, but I was limited on how much I could bring home. If you look closely, each one has a small flaw. It is believed that only God is perfect, so each piece of pottery must have an intentional flaw."

"They're amazing. Do you mind if I pick one up?"

He gave me a *go-ahead* wave from the kitchen. "Feel free. I have way too many."

"Why did you buy so much?" I asked, turning one of the pieces over in my hands. They were crude and refined at the same time. Fascinating.

"I had a fiancé at the time, but when I came home, I discovered she'd found somebody else."

"I'm sorry to hear that."

He nodded. "So was I. But it was a while ago. Feels like the distant past."

I grabbed a seat at the kitchen counter and watched Colton making dinner, moving around the kitchen in nothing but loose sweatpants hanging low on his hips, confidently mixing, chopping, and tasting.

Shit. How was it that a guy like him was single? Or any of these guys, really?

Over in the living room, Logan was tinkering with a guitar, and Theo was setting up a chess game. They led full, satisfying lives, and the things I knew I'd miss if I lived in the middle of nowhere meant nothing to them.

That's when I began to realize how silly the things I thought important were—pretty clothes, good haircuts, a fancy condo. Like foreign currency, those things had no value up here. They simply weren't needed.

Was this a lesson Uncle Bo wanted me to learn?

I shook my head to get that thought out of it. Uncle Bo couldn't know anything about me. There was just no way.

And yet it felt like he did.

"Hey, Colton, do you have any salad? I could really go for some fresh greens."

Logan snorted from across the room. "Ava, we go into town about once a month. That means for the first couple weeks we have fresh produce. After that, we eat the kinds of things that store well, like potatoes and carrots and some canned goods.

He must have seen my face fall because he put down his guitar and came over, putting his arm around me.

As if no one else were in the room, he bent down to kiss me. "I guess you'll have to wait on the salad till you get back to the city. Or, stay here two weeks with us, until we stock up again."

Hmmm. Was he saying he wanted me to split? Or stick around?

And did it really matter?

This was just a quick getaway to iron out the inheritance Bo had left me. Nothing more, nothing less.

I mean, it was a business trip when you really got down to it, and getting rid of his cabin was a transaction that, the sooner it happened, the better.

But still. Logan had hinted that I should stick around. Should I take that as a compliment? Or was he only teasing?

Dinner was delicious, just as it was the first time I'd dined with them and Colton had cooked. Christ, was there anything they couldn't do, and do well?

And aside from the obvious reasons, I wasn't even sure why they were spending time with me. Perhaps it was out of obligation, as Bo's niece? I brought nothing to the table, literally and figuratively, that could be of value or interest to them.

Even my homemade bread was a disaster.

My thoughts whipsawed back and forth until I was dizzy. First, I wanted to convince myself that the guys liked me, thought I was a cool chick, and maybe even wanted to see more of me. But at the same time I didn't see how they could possibly have any respect for me, a city girl without an ounce of useful knowledge about getting by in the mountains. I was more of a burden than anything.

Theo tapped my arm. "Ava? You all right?"

I took a deep breath. "I am. Sorry. I was lost in thought."

He ran his fingers through his facial scruff. It was so damn sexy with his dark blond hair. "I see. I was kind of hoping we'd worn you out."

No big surprise, a searing heat started at the bottom of my neck and in about five seconds had my face on fire. I didn't even have to look in the mirror to know I was bright red.

I didn't even know why.

Another reason they shouldn't want to hang out with me. I had no game.

But I could do my best to hide it.

I stretched my arms, then covered my mouth for a small yawn. "Why I do believe you did wear me out. I was hoping I did the same thing to you."

Colton nodded. "You did, baby. You sure as hell did."

Wow. Now I was *baby*?

Logan put his hands on the table. "Ava, I know you'd probably rather walk home over the almost-finished bridge, but I suggest you let me give you a ride home." He shot Theo a look.

"Hey now, that bridge is nearly done. I got… distracted today and pulled off task." He looked my way and winked.

I couldn't help but giggle. "Yeah, blame it on me, Logan. I pulled your man off the job. But I promise never to do it again."

Theo's head snapped in my direction. "You'd better not mean that." He laughed.

Of course, I didn't. He just didn't know that yet.

23

LOGAN MEYER

"Thanks for the ride home, Logan."

It was all I could do to not stare at her lips and remember how beautifully she'd sucked my dick a few hours earlier.

God help me.

The bit of light shining from the cabin's windows made its way to the cab of my truck, illuminating Ava's pretty face as I pulled up in front.

Fuck, I wanted to grab her hair again... "You're welcome. It was a fun... night."

Jesus. Was it ever.

She giggled nervously. I didn't blame her. She didn't know where she stood with us. 'Course we didn't know where we stood with her, either.

She placed her hand on the car door handle but didn't pull it. Was that hesitation perhaps a signal that the evening wasn't over quite yet?

I opened my own door to test my theory. "How 'bout I walk you to the door? Which, by the way, now not only stays closed when you shut it but also... get this... *locks.*"

She leaned back on the headrest and her laughter filled the truck. "That's so awesome. Seriously. You know, Logan, it might seem trivial to other people, but having an operational door and lock has just improved my life about one hundred percent."

I could think of other ways I'd like to improve her life, given the chance.

As soon as I'd rounded the front of the truck, I took her hand and led her up the cabin's newly repaired front steps. Inserting the key into the new lock, I pushed the door open and flicked on the light.

"I cannot believe how much you got done today, Logan. You are amazing. I'll write you a check as payment. Or do you prefer cash?"

I didn't give a shit about the money—I couldn't stop thinking about what she looked like naked...

I waved my hands. "Please stop worrying about that. You're not paying me."

"What? Wait a minute. We agreed—"

"Hold on. We never agreed. You just thought we did."

She rolled her eyes. "C'mon. You have to let me pay you—"

I didn't want to hear anything more about money so, without a word, I pulled her to me and pressed my lips against hers. What was it about this woman, whose chosen path was so different from where I was in my own life, that drew us to each other? We had nothing in common—but everything in common.

She lived in the city, I lived in the mountains. She drank good wine. I drank homemade moonshine. Yet we were both working our way through life, hoping to find meaning and connection.

That sounded more alike than not, if you asked me.

And we sure as hell were compatible with our clothes off… But, as good as her lips felt against mine, I needed to get back home. It was fucking killing me, but as much as I wanted to hang out, it didn't seem like a good idea. She'd be gone in a couple days anyway. I'd probably never see her again.

Releasing her, I kissed her forehead.

"Where are you going?" she asked sadly.

Uh oh.

"I was thinking I'd better head out. I have an early morning. I have some things to do around the house, and then I have to get back over here. I can't be a slacker with my biggest client."

She laughed. "Well then, if I'm the client, I'm also your boss."

"I hadn't looked at it that way." Shit. This could be fun. "What does the boss lady want?"

Amused, she tilted her head. "Why don't you tuck me in? Talk to me for a few minutes until I get tired."

Was she goddamn kidding? I'd talk to her all night long if that meant I'd get to spend time with her.

But I'd play it cool. It's just the way I was.

"Sure. I'll hang for a bit."

I waited in the living room until she called me. She was tucked into Bo's gazillion dollar bed with the sheets pulled up to her neck. I sat on the edge of the bed next to her and realized she wasn't exaggerating.

It was an awesome fucking bed.

I bounced up and down. "Wow. This is nice. You weren't kidding."

She laughed. "Isn't it the weirdest thing? The man was living with no bathroom, leaks in his roof, busted out front steps, and yet he had the king of all mattresses. So bizarre."

I thought back to the last time I'd seen Bo, just before he'd left for Key West. He was no spring chicken, but he had a full head of thick, silvery hair, and was about as buff as any man I'd ever known. When he smiled, which was often, the lines around his eyes deepened, giving him even more character than he already had. I couldn't lie. I was going to miss him.

"Your uncle was a special guy. Like a combination friend-slash-dad."

Ava sat up in bed. "Really? I had no idea."

I nodded. "Much nicer guy than my own dad, who still blames me for his business failing." I laughed weakly.

"Do you speak to him often? Your dad?"

"I called to check in a few days ago. My mom isn't well. But it seems like every time I call, even though it's only to speak with her, I always get stuck listening to a snarky remark or two from my dad."

She reached for my hand. "Sorry to hear that. You don't deserve to be treated that way."

I turned from my spot and her long brunette hair spilled over the shoulder straps of whatever it was she had on under the sheets. So, before I left, I peeled the covers down to see her hard nipples poking through a thin top. I smoothed over one of them with the open palm of my hand. She gasped and reached for my neck, and I kissed her again.

But I excused myself in short order. I wanted nothing more than to stick around, but I had to get back and talk to Colton and Theo before they all went to bed. Our relationships were key to our existence up on Deep Water Mountain, and I needed to make sure a beautiful woman named Ava wasn't endangering that.

24

LOGAN MEYER

"Yo. Guys."

Colton looked up from his reading. "Hey. I figured you'd probably stay over there for the night."

I grabbed a seat on the sofa next to Theo, who was still trying to teach himself chess.

"Nah. I wanted to get back here and talk to you all. About Ava."

I had their attention, now.

"What's up, Logan?" Theo asked.

I struggled to find the right words, and before I did, Colton pretty much found them for me.

He slapped his hand on his thigh. "Holy shit. Logan, you'd never done anything like what we did today with Ava, have you?"

I shot him a glance. "Actually, no, I hadn't. Are you saying you have?"

He looked at his brother, who looked at me.

"Yeah, man. We've done menage plenty of times. Never had a third guy join in but today's session was fucking hot," Theo said. "She was catatonic, she was so worked up."

"You guys are totally cool with it?"

Colton started to say something, then stopped, then started again. "Are… you saying you're not? I mean, I think we all like her. Am I right?"

I nodded. "Yeah. I want to make sure this doesn't get in the way of us three. We have a good setup here on the mountain, and Ava is only passing through. I want to make sure there's no weirdness."

"Dude, are you wanting to date her or something?" Theo asked, incredulous.

"I… I don't know," I stammered. "It's not actually possible, when it comes down to it. She's leaving soon. But it seems like you guys feel the same way."

Colton nodded. "I think she's awesome. If she were sticking around, I'd definitely like to get to know her better."

"Logan, have you ever shared a woman?" Theo asked.

"I haven't. Obviously." I laughed.

"Colt and I have. It's pretty freaking amazing. I think that if Ava's going to spend any amount of time up here, we should see if she's into it. That is, unless you feel like you'd want her all to yourself."

Colton laughed. "Yeah, and if that's the case, then *game on.*"

Jesus. Would they really want to compete for her?

But there was no reason to. If I could get my head around the idea of sharing, then that could prevent a lot of potential problems.

"I just don't want this to get in the way of our usual routines. Like maybe we should say no messing around during the day, since we all have a lot to do."

Theo slapped me on the back. "Okay, bro, you're telling me that if the lovely Ava came traipsing over here for some sexy time, you'd tell her you had to finish chopping wood first?

I had to laugh at that. "Yeah. I see what you mean."

"I can't believe you never did any menage or anything. You've never been with two girls?" Theo asked.

Jesus. I felt like I was fourteen again and everyone else had started fucking around except for me. "Back off, dickhead. Some of us are a bit more traditional than others."

I stood to head to my room. I needed some alone time.

"Yeah, keep telling yourself that, mister vanilla. But don't worry, Logan. My brother and I are happy to usher you into a new world of sensuality. As long as the lovely Ava wants in."

I flipped off their good-natured ribbing just to be obnoxious and headed to bed.

My eyes were feeling heavy when I climbed under the covers a few minutes later, but I wasn't ready for sleep. All I could see was Ava's face, and expression when I'd come in her mouth.

Without realizing it, I'd begun stroking myself. While my own hand was a far cry from Ava's ministrations, imagining the curves of her body made my dick so hard it was painful.

In my imagination, I pulled back the covers on her bed, just as she'd been lying that night, and found her in the same nightgown she'd answered the door in when I'd arrived to go to work on the house.

I lifted the hem enough to see her pink pussy, and ran one finger through her lips to find them already soaked.

When I pushed the nightie up the rest of the way, she helped me pull it off, and started working on my own clothes. While she did, I teased her breasts, her nipples hard and pointed.

Fuck, if I didn't slow down, I'd explode in my hand in seconds.

I pictured myself putting her on her knees with her ass in the air so I could get a full view of her most private parts. After pumping her pussy full with my fingers, I lined up my dick to bury myself all the way to her core.

If I'd really been with Ava at that moment, I would have tried to hold my cum, but because it was just me, and I was tired as hell, I exploded into the palm of my hand.

Fuck me. I hoped for more stamina when faced with the real thing—with my dick deep inside Ava instead of my hand.

25

AVA STONE

"Wow. Smells great, Ava."

"Glad you like it, Colt."

Bo's cabin had probably never smelled so delicious.

The general store might not have niceties like bagels, but they did have white bread, milk, and eggs. So, I whipped up a giant batch of French toast and placed a pile on not three but *four* plates—because, to hell with that stupid no-carb rule—and drizzled warm maple syrup over everything and added a sprinkling of diced strawberries.

I wasn't sure who was more excited, me or the guys. I hadn't had French toast in probably ten years.

"Everybody have a seat," I said, pretending to make sure everyone had a fork, knife, and napkin, but really checking out the three very hot men whom I'd been with less than twenty-four hours earlier. What an experience that had been and one I'd never forget, that was for sure.

Probably one I wouldn't repeat, either.

As much as I might like to.

It's not every day a girl finds herself in the company of three gorgeous, strapping mountain men who were also passionate as hell.

I'd certainly never find this at home, living my 'city life,' such as it were.

It's funny what a new point of view will do. Since I'd been up at Bo's cabin, I'd been looking at, well, everything, from a different perspective. Like rotating a vase of flowers to see what was on the other side. So far, there were some things I liked, and some that I didn't.

I'd hardly be going home an entirely different person. I wasn't naïve enough to think a few days roughing it in a mountain cabin would wipe someone's slate clean, nor was I looking for that. At the end of the day, I'd still be the same person. What was becoming clear, however, was that by 'rotating my vase,' the sunflowers on the far side were equally as nice as the roses I'd placed in front because I'd always thought roses were 'best.'

I poured everyone coffee and joined them at the table, where three hungry men dove into a homemade breakfast.

"Oh my god. Baby, these are great," Colton said, his mouth half-full.

Baby. I was *baby*.

Theo and Logan nodded in agreement.

He was right. They were heavenly.

But what was even better was knowing I'd made something the guys were enjoying so thoroughly.

"This is good, if I don't say so myself. You guys have had me over a couple times now. I was trying to think of a way to say thank you, you know, return the favor, but it's not the easiest thing to do in Bo's cabin, rustic as it is. But something simple like French toast, I can pull off. Anything more complicated, you would probably be out of luck."

He looked around. "I haven't been here in a while. I think I missed the last poker game before Bo left for the winter. When he lived here, I didn't think twice about how… rough the place was. But your being here is such a contrast that it's pretty evident now."

Theo raised his finger. "But this place has great potential. It's small but a good layout that doesn't waste space."

"If only you had a bathroom." Logan laughed.

Ugh. The thorn in my side. He was right. If only. But it just didn't seem to be something I'd be able to afford.

"Speaking of your… hospitality," I stammered, "I thought we could talk about what happened yesterday."

Their faces grew serious, and they set their forks down. Well, Theo set his down after his brother nudged him.

"I'd never done anything like that before," I admitted sheepishly.

Theo guffawed. "You're not the only one," he said, looking at Logan.

"You guys have?" I asked, looking between the brothers.

They looked at each other and shrugged. "I thought everyone did that sort of thing from time to time."

I could see why he thought that. It was hands-down the sexiest thing I'd ever experienced in my life.

"And did you like it? Or are you letting us down easily because it was a one-off thing?" Colton teased.

He saw right through me.

"I… I wanted to say I really enjoyed it. Like, seriously. It was beyond hot."

Logan shrugged. "Too bad you're leaving, Ava. I gotta tell you, we were talking about you last night."

Oh shit. That didn't sound good.

"We agreed if you were sticking around, we'd all like to date you."

My thoughts whipsawed between *oh goody, they like me*, and in what world did *three friends all date the same woman?*

I swallowed hard and squirmed in my seat. It was a strange sensation to be uncomfortable and turned on at the same time.

But while my heart was pounding and boob sweat was starting to collect, I also experienced that tingling, spreading fire in my core—the kind that tickled the belly and made your hair feel like it was standing on end.

I was so screwed.

"I… wow… thank you. I don't know what to say. But I'm flattered. What a compliment. My living arrangements aside, how do you all date one woman?

Theo looked at his brother, who gave him the go ahead

to speak on his behalf. "We share. People do it all the time."

I laughed. "Sounds… like a harem. Three men and me."

Which sounded pretty freaking awesome.

"But for as long as you're around, we could continue to have fun," Logan said. "We have a lot of work to do during the day, so I suggested we keep together time to the evenings—"

I caught Colton and Theo exchanging looks.

Exactly.

Was he fucking kidding?

"Logan, that is the silliest thing I've ever heard," I interrupted.

He threw his hands in the air. "Sounds like I've been overruled. But guys, if the new chickens arrive and their coop isn't built, you will not be throwing blame my way."

Theo faked shock. "No, Logan. We would *never* do that."

"Don't worry, Logan. We can have fun *and* get the chicken coop built," Colton said.

Logan shrugged and brought his plate to the sink. "Okay guys. Everybody needs to clear out now so I can get to work on the house."

At the sound of that, I jumped up too. I didn't want anything getting in the way of Logan's work. In fact, I had an idea.

"Hey, can I walk with you guys back to your house and use the facilities?" I flirtatiously asked the brothers.

"Sure, especially since the bridge is done now," Theo said.

Colton smirked, his dimple making its rare appearance. "But don't forget, Bro, that the troll under the bridge is back and Ava will have to pay to cross."

I set the rest of the dishes in the sink to wash later, excited about using a real bathroom. "How much is the bridge toll?" I teased.

Theo took my hand. "It's expensive. Very, very expensive."

WHEN WE REACHED THE HOUSE, the guys grabbed what they needed for the day to hunt wild animals and chop down wood and shit, and took off, leaving me alone. Since no one was around, I decided to take advantage of my access to the facilities and took a nice, long, leisurely shower. I hadn't asked whether I could do that, but I seriously doubted they'd care. Afterwards, walking around in the robe I found hanging on the bathroom door, I decided to call my boss.

"Ava. How's life in the mountains? Have you started wearing flannel and letting the hair grow out on your legs yet?" she asked.

"Very funny," I said, forcing myself to laugh.

Less than a week earlier, I might have made the same sort of joke, assuming that people who lived in the mountains were somehow less sophisticated than us 'city folks.' But now that stereotyping chafed me.

As if I'd let my grooming slip when I had three guys

who were going to be running their hands—and other things—all over me.

"Hey, would it be okay if I stayed longer? I have my computer. I could write some press releases for you. Stuff like that."

I'd noticed Logan on a laptop. They must have a decent internet connection, unlike Bo's house.

Maybe I could poach their internet along with their nice bathroom?

"Actually, that's a great idea, Ava. We have a bunch we need written and you're perfect for that."

We went back and forth about what needed to be done and said our goodbyes.

"Remember, Ava, you are still entitled to all that vacation time you've never used. I appreciate your getting the work done but I hope you'll find some way to relax as well. It's hard to get the city out of our systems."

Funny. I'd been thinking it was going to be hard to get the mountains out of my system.

26

AVA STONE

"Well, look who it is."

I smiled at Colton as I made my way down the last of the path leading to the pond where he was fishing.

"I thought you were the big hunter. Fishing seems too... mellow for you. Like not mean and manly enough."

He laughed. "Is that how you look at me? Mean and manly? Damn. I'm gonna have to work on that."

Actually, he didn't have to work on anything. He was perfect as is. Not that I was going to tell him that.

"Whatcha doing down here at the pond? I thought you didn't go exploring in the woods. You know, because they're so dangerous."

Smart ass.

"I still think they are dangerous. But I'm feeling more

144

comfortable, and besides, I need to do something with my time."

Since woodworking hadn't gone all that well.

He reeled in his line and set his fishing pole aside. "Aren't you taking off soon? I thought you weren't going to stay up here on the mountain."

I hoped he'd be happy with what I was about to say.

"I talked to my boss. I can do some work remotely. But she really wants me to use some of my vacation time to relax and enjoy myself."

His eyebrows rose, and he nodded slowly. "No kidding. You don't actually hate it up here?"

"What? Are you kidding? What makes you think I hate it?"

He smiled with the corner of his mouth, and his dimple popped into view.

Damn him.

"I don't know. You haven't seemed to enjoy it up here all that much. I can't blame you, having to rough it at Bo's place, especially when you're not used to that sort of thing. It's a shock to the system."

He had a point. And I appreciated his understanding.

"You're right. It hasn't exactly been easy. But on the other hand, no one is holding a gun to my head, making me stay. So since it's my decision to stick around, I guess I have no right to complain, huh?"

He laughed. "You know what? Complaining never helped anyone. No matter how good it feels for a moment or two. So, I don't do it. Learned that in the Army. The guys—and women—who learned to roll with the punches were a lot better off."

He looked out over the pond, lost in his thoughts.

"Hey, Colton, how cold is that water?"

"What? This pond water? It's pretty cold. I mean, it's fed from snow melt, so even on the hottest summer day, it's not very warm. Why? You want to go swimming?"

I shrugged. "I don't know. I was thinking about it."

"Mmmm. I don't advise it."

Colton was about to learn that when you tell me not to do something... I usually do it.

I jumped to my feet and kicked off my sneakers, followed by my T-shirt and jeans. There I stood in my pink thong and lacey white bra.

Colton waved his hands as if to warn me away from the water. I'm telling you, Ava, it's cold..."

I dipped a toe off the tiny pier they'd built. He wasn't kidding. It was fucking freezing. But that wasn't going to stop me from having some fun.

After all, I wasn't Uncle Bo's niece for nothing.

I held my breath, stepped off the pier, and jumped into the water.

My shriek must have been heard for miles. Freezing water will do that to you.

Up to my waist in the cold, my body exploded in goosebumps. It was the kind of temperature that was so freezing, it almost felt like it was burning.

Back on the edge of the pond, Colton stood with his mouth hanging open.

"C'mon," I yelled, splashing water his way. "Don't be a chicken. Get in here."

He narrowed his eyes at me. "Did you just call me a chicken?"

I jumped up and down in the waist-high water, trying to generate some warmth. But I had a feeling that as soon as Colton was in the water, we'd be generating all sorts of heat.

"I might have said chicken. It, um, slipped out. Sorry. What are you gonna do about it, anyway?" I teased.

Hands on his hips, he shook his head, laughing. Then, he pulled off his boots and removed his jeans and flannel shirt, leaving him standing there in his boxers. He ran off the end of the pier and tucked his arms and legs into a cannonball.

Heading straight for me.

I screamed and moved out of the way in time for him to create a splash so big he soaked the rest of me, including my hair.

Damn. I'd planned on keeping my hair dry.

"You jerk!" I laughed, using all my strength to splash a wall of water in his direction.

It was like being a kid again. I hadn't had a splash fight in... well, I didn't know how long.

Finally, he lunged for me and I didn't move fast enough. He spun me around and picked me up around the waist. With my arms and legs flailing, he carried me to the pond's embankment and set me on my feet.

I immediately started shivering. "I... I was having fun in there," I stuttered, my teeth chattering.

"Fun? You practically have icicles hanging from your ears." He grabbed my hand. "Come over here, in the sun. We'll dry off."

It was slightly warmer, but I was still shivering.

"You're going to have to take the rest of your clothes off. They are keeping you wet," he said, as he pushed his boxers down to his ankles and stepped out of them. "It's the only way to get dry."

I reached behind myself and unhooked my bra, then slipped my panties down like he'd done his boxers and there we stood, facing each other in a beautiful, grassy clearing with the sun shining on us.

He rubbed his hands up and down my arms to warm me up. "Why the hell did you jump in that pond?"

I smiled coyly. "I didn't really think it would be that bad."

"I warned you..."

I pressed my fingers against his lips, interrupting him. "Yes, you did. And I didn't listen. I rarely do."

He moved my fingers from his lips. "I knew you were the stubborn type. If you weren't, you would have bailed on Bo's cabin a long time ago."

He turned my hand over, kissing my palm. His gaze caught mine, and he kissed my forearm. He looked at me again, and planted another kiss in the crease of my elbow. I tingled from one end of my body to the other, and hoped my wobbly legs would keep me upright.

By the time his lips reached my neck, my eyes had fluttered closed and I'd rested my arms around his neck. The length of his body against mine was intoxicating with both its warmth and pure strength. He was pulling me into his hold, and there was nothing I could do to resist.

Not that I wanted to.

He leaned next to my ear. "I think I need to fuck you."

I gasped. Not because I was surprised, but because of the intensity with which he spoke the words. He was so authoritative. And demanding.

And freaking sexy.

And now my legs really were failing me.

He lowered me to the soft grass and lay me back, hovering and kissing my neck, breasts, and stomach. I scraped my fingernails through his short, neat hair, and he groaned.

"Hold on a sec."

He walked back to where he'd left his jeans on the ground. Reaching into a pocket, he retrieved a condom.

That's what I'm talking about.

Positioning himself between my legs, he sheathed his hard cock and pressed it into my opening. I was wild with desire, and if he wasn't inside me in seconds, I was sure I'd lose my mind. I wanted him badly and would do anything to have him.

"Are you ready for me, baby?" he rasped.

I nodded. "Yeah. I am, Colton."

He entered me slowly, and when he stretched me to my limit, I dug my nails into his back to handle the initial sting. He waited for me to adjust, and then began to pump me slowly.

"I... I need more..." I gasped, wanting to beg but holding myself back.

"Yeah? You want more dick, Ava?"

His dirty words intensified the pressure building in my core. I grabbed his ass and pulled him into me, hard.

"I do, please. Please, Colton," I whispered.

He began to piston me so hard I grabbed the grass under me for purchase, pulling up tufts and staining my hands green. But it didn't matter, because an orgasm was rolling over me, leaving me gasping for air and tossing my head from side to side on the ground.

When a second orgasm smashed over me, Colton began to groan. I opened my eyes to watch the cords on his neck strain. He squeezed his eyes tight and gritted his teeth, exploding with a thunderous groan, expanding inside me one last time before his release.

He collapsed with his head on my chest, trying to catch his breath as I rubbed my hands through his hair and over his back. I'd been watching Colton since I'd arrived on the mountain. He was impossible to turn away from—strong and sleek, like an exotic animal. He was quiet and thoughtful most of the time, not speaking unless he really had something to say.

So different from his fun-loving brother Theo, and protective friend Logan.

What a threesome they made.

What a foursome we all made.

Jesus, I was so fucked. Literally and figuratively.

27

THEO PAYNE

"Hey, man. Need any help?"

Logan looked over my way. "Yeah. Hold this end of the measuring tape."

Colton and Ava were off in the woods somewhere, hopefully enjoying the hell out of each other, so I figured I'd wander over to Bo's cabin to see what Logan was working on.

"You know, we can probably fit a bathroom right here," he said, taking the dimensions of a large storage closet.

I was still baffled as to why Bo never built out a bathroom in all his years in the cabin. But we'd never get an answer to that now.

"That would be great. Ava would be thrilled. And

maybe she'd stick around for longer, if she didn't have to come over to our place to pee all the time."

Logan looked at me with a play stern expression. "You'd like that wouldn't you? For her to stay longer?"

"Ha-ha. Tell me you wouldn't like exactly the same."

He shook his head. "I don't know what it is about her, but she's gotten under my skin, that's for goddamn sure. You know, she's a pain in the ass, but perfect at the same time. It's so fucking weird. I've never known anyone like it."

Wow. Logan was smitten. He wasn't the only one, though. And it was my sincere hope that we could work through all three of us dating her. If she stayed on the mountain, that was.

Which didn't seem very likely.

"She's special, all right."

Logan started knocking on walls to see which were load bearing. "I think this may actually work, if you can believe it. With a minimal amount of digging we can tie into the main coming off the well, and build a nice little bathroom."

I watched Logan in his element. He was a builder at heart, and the rift with his father had pushed him out of that business. He was never happier than when he was creating something habitable with his hands. I'd learned a lot from him in the short time he'd lived with Colton and me.

"It's still a big project, Logan. I'm not sure Ava has the money to pay you for the work and materials."

He threw me a side-eye. "I'm not charging her. Are you kidding? That would be a serious douchebag move."

Regardless of Ava's relationship with us, I didn't think she'd be comfortable with Logan taking on such a big project for nothing.

"You sure she'll go for that?" I asked.

He ran a hand over his bald head like he always did when he was thinking. "I know how I can handle that. I'll position it as if I were doing it for Bo. To sort of honor his memory. He was a good guy."

I laughed. "You're gonna honor someone's memory by building a bathroom?"

He shrugged. "Yeah, well, that does sound kind of stupid. But I was trying to think of some way for Ava to let herself off the hook for paying. She's not the kind of person who expects things for free. She wants to pay her way."

"Do you think she'll sell the place?"

He shook his head. "Hard to tell. But you know, I can only put so much time into this. We have to get back to stockpiling wood for the winter, and get the chicken coop finished. So if you're here to help, I'm happy to put you to work."

"I'm all yours, boss. Just tell me I'll be on the demolition team when the time comes to tear down that outhouse."

Ava would be especially happy to see that thing gone.

Of course, since I volunteered to help, Logan gave me the shit job of starting to dig to install the pipes needed to bring water to the bathroom. He ran out to visit a friend who renovated homes to see if he had any decent bathroom fixtures he could get a good price on.

It felt good to work up a sweat, and the meditative exertion had me thinking non-stop of Ava. The more I thought about my discomfort with only ever having lived on the mountain, and learned about her life, it occurred to me that maybe I wasn't missing much after all. It seemed I had all I needed right here in Deep Water.

Especially since she'd come on the scene.

"What's for dinner tonight, Colton?"

He looked at Ava, sitting at the kitchen counter, with a grin that let me know they'd done more than simply walk in the woods that afternoon.

And I thought that was fucking wonderful.

"I am making a curry, one version with chicken and vegetables, and another with just vegetables for my pain in the ass brother."

I flipped him off. "I can hear you over here, Colt."

He waved me away. "You'll get over it, Bro."

"You guys are so funny," Ava said.

"Ha. You should have seen us when we were kids. We'd beat the crap out of each other."

Ava walked over to Logan and me and took a seat opposite my chess game. "So, guys. I've been thinking."

We looked up. Was she going to drop a bomb?

"I talked to my boss today. She told me I could hang out here for longer."

Holy shit.

"That's great news," I said, picking up Ava and twirling her around.

Logan, usually more reserved than me, lit up with a huge grin.

Ava exhaled loudly. "I'm so glad you guys think it's a good idea. I mean, if it weren't for all of you, there'd be no reason to stay on the mountain. I don't know what I would have done with the cabin. I could never afford that other contractor. I guess I would have had to sell the place for pennies just to get rid of it. Kind of a sad legacy for my uncle."

Logan leaned forward, elbows on knees, after I'd set Ava back down on the sofa. "I wanted to talk to you about that, Ava. I liked your Uncle Bo. All us guys did. He was a crazy bastard, and he was good to us. Because of that, I want to fix up the cabin in his memory. At no cost to you."

Ava's mouth dropped open. "Oh no. No, I can't let you do that. You're so kind, but I would never take advantage."

Logan held his hands up. "It's not like that. You are not taking advantage. I want to do this. We all want to do this. Think of it as something for Bo. Like you said, for his legacy."

She clapped a hand over her mouth and her eyes got watery, like I knew they would. She was so fucking cute.

"Oh my god. Thank you. Thank all of you. You've been so good to me. I don't know how I'll ever return the favor."

"That's kind of the point, sweetie. You don't have to return the favor. This is something nice I want to do."

She sniffled, pretending she wasn't about to cry. "I... I'm running to the restroom. Be right back," she said, jumping out of her seat and heading down the hall.

I slapped Logan on the back. "You handled that well, my friend. Made a nice person very happy."

"Bo was good to us, so it's nice to keep it in the family. Isn't it?"

28

THEO PAYNE

I HAD TO SAY, MY BROTHER'S CURRY DISHES WERE EPIC. BUT, as good as they were, I couldn't wait for dinner to be over so play time could start.

Seemed Ava couldn't wait, either.

She'd barely finished what was on her plate when she started gathering the dinner dishes and putting them in the sink. In fact, I still had food on mine when she whisked it away. I caught Logan stifling a laugh.

No one was complaining.

"Go ahead to the living room," she said, waving us away. "I have some after dinner drinks to serve."

After dinner drinks? Jesus, our little world had changed a lot in a few days' time.

I grabbed my usual seat in front of the chess board,

157

thinking I'd occupy myself with it while Ava did her thing. But what was funny was, I could only stare at the pieces on the board. I was so preoccupied I couldn't even remember what each one was for.

Cripes, how that woman got me worked up.

Unable to focus, I looked up to find Colton strumming his guitar quietly in the corner, and Logan flipping through one of the old Playboys Ava had given us from Bo's stash.

"Hey, Logan, having fun over there? Do you need some private time to relieve yourself?"

He shook his head and put the magazine aside. "These old Playboys are so funny. They're almost quaint. What a great reminder of Bo."

Ava joined us with a bottle and 4 glasses on a tray.

We had a *tray?*

Colton stopped his strumming. "I love that Ava gets bequeathed a cabin, and we get the vintage Playboys. Something about that is just *so* Bo."

She served us each a small glass of thick, red liquid. I wanted to call it wine but it was darker. And thicker.

"You are so lucky to have really known him," Ava sighed. "I hadn't seen him since I was a kid. I barely remember anything about him aside from he was nice and always had spearmint candies."

"Are you gonna tell us what this is, Ava?" Colton asked.

She held her glass up in a toast. "This is a very nice bottle of port that I found in Uncle Bo's house. I figure someone gave it to him and he never got around to drinking it. Here's to Bo."

We raised our glasses, and I took my first sip. Turns out, it was a lot like wine, stronger.

"This stuff is great. I've never had port," I said.

Colton leaned back, glass in hand, looking very happy. "Bro, you need to get out more."

I shrugged.

"I don't know about that," Ava said. "This is a pretty freaking awesome place. I don't think anyone has to apologize for holing up on Deep Water Mountain. The more I think about it, the more I realize the other stuff going on in the world isn't *all that*."

Holy shit. Had she really just said that?

The corner of Logan's mouth crooked up, and he nodded. "You're liking it up here are ya? Outhouse and all?"

She sipped her port. "Let me tell you, the whole thing would have been unbearable if not for all of you. And I've used your bathroom probably half the time anyway." She laughed. "So, I've not suffered too badly."

"Speaking of bathrooms," Logan said, glancing at me, "Theo and I have made some major progress in the last couple days and expect the bulk of the work to be done tomorrow."

Ava's eyes widened and she set down her glass to clap her hands. "Are you kidding? Oh my god, that's amazing."

Logan continued. "I have a request to make. Don't go back over there until we tell you that you can. We want to surprise you with something as close to finished as possible."

She jumped out of her chair and ran to kiss Logan.

But before she could get away to kiss me, he pulled her to his lap.

"Well, hello," she crooned.

With one swift move, he gathered her hands behind her back and held them in one of his. When she realized she was more or less pinned, she squirmed, trying to get free.

But not too hard.

She rolled her eyes. "Oh, help!" she said in a fake-high voice.

Logan fake-furrowed his brow. "I've got her now boys. What shall we do with her?"

Ava bit her lip to keep from giggling.

"Logan," Colton said, rising from his chair, "I've got a few ideas." He walked over to where Ava was perched on Logan's lap and put his hand under her chin, tilting her head to look up at him.

But she averted her eyes.

She was good. She knew just how to play.

"Look at me."

Without a word, she shook her head slowly and kept looking down.

And now my dick was getting hard.

Colton tilted her head further up, squeezing her face harder, probably to the point of discomfort, and distorting her pretty features.

"Mmmm," she moaned. But she finally met his gaze.

"Trying to think of what I might do with you, pretty lady," he said, starting to unbutton his jeans with his free hand.

She squirmed again.

"Logan, hold her, dammit."

He shifted in his seat, probably suffering from a massive hard-on like I was.

"I got her, Colt. She ain't going anywhere."

Colton pulled his hard cock out from his pants and rubbed it over her lips.

"What do you want, Ava?" he asked.

She mumbled something.

"What? We can't hear you."

"I said, I want to suck your cock," she snapped.

Okay. She was playing the brat.

"Open," he demanded.

She slowly parted her lips, looking up at him with the most defiant stare I'd ever seen.

Fucking awesome.

He pushed his cock into her mouth until she coughed. He pulled back out.

"You want me to stop?" he asked.

With watering eyes, she shook her head wildly. "No. Please no."

29

AVA STONE

COLTON SHOVED HIS COCK IN MY MOUTH ONE LAST TIME, AS if he were putting on a show for everyone, and with a roar, spurted hot cum down my throat. I sputtered and swallowed, and let the rest run down my chin and onto my breasts, exposed because Logan had pulled up my shirt and bra.

Theo, in the meantime, had wrestled my jeans down below my ass and pushed my legs open to finger my pussy. He ran his fingers through my wet excitement, stopping to massage my clit, and then entered me with exploring fingers.

And I was still sitting on Logan's knee with my arms held behind my back.

Cripes. These guys. So mind-blowingly hot. I'd been

on the verge of coming all by myself throughout the entire dinner. Every time I looked at one of them, heat surged through my core, leaving me soaked and throbbing. At one point, I was so lost in thought about Colton's fucking me by the pond that Logan had to snap his fingers to bring my attention back to the room.

Finally, when dinner wasn't even fully over, I cleared the table. I just couldn't wait any longer for these men to have their hands on me. I was obsessed with pleasing them and had to admit, was ready to do anything they wanted.

When Colton pulled out of my mouth, Logan and Theo laid me down on the living room rug and finished removing my clothes.

But they didn't remove theirs. In fact, Colton tucked himself back into his jeans, and zipped up.

"Sit in the middle of the floor," Theo said, pointing.

Had they done this before? They were so in sync.

I sat on my knees in the middle of the floor while everyone else remained standing. They moved around me so they were evenly spaced, forming a circle around their prey. I looked in front of me and over each shoulder, keeping an eye on them, wondering what was next.

Colton had just come in my mouth, so I guessed it was the other guys' turns?

"Move your knees apart, now."

I followed Theo's instructions.

"Very nice. Now we have a perfect view of your pussy and ass."

My heart was thudding, and if someone didn't do

something soon, I was going to start playing with myself, I was that desperate for release.

They circled me like I was prey, eyeing me greedily and degradingly, as if I weren't even human.

And I loved it.

"Which do you like best, my friends? Her pussy or ass?" Theo asked.

Logan stopped in front of me, rubbing his chin. "Hmmm. I don't know."

"I thought you were an ass man, Logan."

Logan was an *ass man*? That kinky fucker.

He nodded. "Yeah. I usually am. But that pussy is so damn pretty."

The way they talked about me, as if I weren't even there, sent me exploding in goosebumps.

"Look at those nipples, getting so hard."

I glanced down at myself.

"Eyes up!" Colton barked.

Holy shit.

"She's smiling. Think she's having fun?" he said.

Logan nodded, walking closer to me. "I think she is. Now show us your pussy, Ava. I have to decide if I want that or your ass."

Oh my god, ass. "I'm not really big on ass stuff—"

"Quiet," Colton demanded.

Logan continued. "Okay. Back to the pussy. Touch yourself down there. Show us what you got."

All right. I could play this game.

Parting my knees wider, I moved a hand between my

legs, running my fingers through my wet folds, first fingering my opening, and moving up to my clit.

"I think I'm gonna need that pussy."

Ohthankgod.

"Her ass is going to take some training."

What?

"Would someone get me a condom?" he asked.

Theo reached in his pocket and tossed one to Logan.

"Okay," he said, gesturing with his chin, "on your hands and knees."

As I did so, he continued to bark instructions. "Ass up. Head down."

Holy shit. Now I was *really* exposed for the whole world to see.

"Looking good, Ava," Theo said.

I heard a belt buckle opening behind me, the rustle of clothing being pushed aside, and the tear of a condom packet. Next, Logan's hands were on my ass cheeks.

He leaned next to my ear. "You ready for me, baby?"

I nodded. Even if I weren't, I would have begged him to fuck me.

And fuck me he did.

I screamed because in one thrust, he was inside me to the hilt. He pulled back out and after teasing me with the head of his dick for a few moments, drove himself balls deep again.

"Look at Logan fucking the shit out of Ava," Colton growled.

Logan reached for my long hair and gathering it into

one hand, gave a gentle tug. "You doing okay, baby?" he asked.

"Mmmm."

"Okay then," he said. "Theo, go do your thing."

"Don't mind if I do."

He lifted my head off the floor. "C'mon. I have something for you to suck, baby."

In seconds, he was in my mouth. They were tag-teaming me again. And I hoped it would never end.

Forget about the cabin, the city, work, my dreams of a nice condo. None of it mattered at that moment. All that did was getting some sort of release, and of course making sure the guys felt good, too.

With Logan behind me and Theo in front, we fell into a rhythm of sucking and fucking, with Colton kicked back on the sofa, smiling and watching. It was unlike anything I'd ever imagined. When Logan thrust into my pussy, it pushed me harder into Theo, and when Theo thrust into my mouth, it pushed me back against Logan.

The familiar throbbing and contracting in my pussy began to build and I knew my orgasm was near. Even with my mouth full, I managed to groan. Sensing how close I was, Logan reached around for my clit and began to rub it. That shit sent me over my edge. I kept sucking Theo but my entire body convulsed in pleasure, energy exploding out of every pore.

I was surprised I didn't freaking ignite.

And as a second orgasm bowled over me, Theo pulled out of my mouth and pressed his cock against my cheek, unloading all over it.

Coated in cum, I bucked my head and screamed. Logan's cock filled me one last time and he roared behind me, shuddering as he pumped his last few drops into me.

Oh. My. God.

Colton stood and, smiling down at me, began to clap his hands. "Nice show, baby. That was about the hottest fucking thing I'd ever seen."

"So glad I could please you," I whispered, totally wiped out. "That was intense," I murmured, falling into Theo's arms.

"Here you go," Logan said, returning from the kitchen with a wet towel and wiping me down.

"I'm exhausted. I don't even think I can walk," I mumbled

Theo bent and scooped me up off the floor. "It's a good thing you're staying here tonight then. I'm taking you to the guest room, which is ready to go."

He tucked me in, and before he could say goodnight, I began to nod off. But as I heard the bedroom door clicking shut, I called out to him.

"Theo. Will you spend the night with me? In here?"

He came back in and kissed me on the forehead. "Sure, baby. Anything you want."

Anything I want. How often did a girl hear those words?

30

AVA STONE

BECAUSE LOGAN HAD EVERYONE WORKING ON MY CABIN and didn't want me coming by yet, I spent the day hanging out at their place. But by early afternoon, I couldn't wait any longer. I skipped out the door and over Theo's new bridge. I was at Uncle Bo's in record time, and as I approached the house, I heard the lovely buzz of building tools.

Yes.

When I'd woken up that morning in the guest bedroom, Theo, who'd spent the night with me, was already gone. By the time I got my butt out of bed, there was nobody left in the house. I'd helped myself to some breakfast, took a long shower, read for a while, and started going stir crazy.

I was like a kid on Christmas morning—dying to see my presents. Or in this case, new bathroom.

I waited outside the cabin for a moment before going in, suddenly struck by a wave of bashfulness due to what had gone down the night before. Our sexy time had been nothing less than mind blowing. In fact, I'd dreamt about it all night long. But there was that nagging little whisper running through my mind, pecking at me with annoying questions like *should you really have done that?* And, *aren't you just going back to the city eventually, anyway?*

Why was I worried? It was true, I'd opened myself up to them, both literally and figuratively. That kind of thing can end up with people getting hurt. But hey, we were all adults and knew the consequences of doing adult things.

And because of that, I pushed it right out of my mind and burst through the door of Uncle Bo's cabin.

"Hello," I called. "I couldn't wait any longer."

I headed to the back corner of the cabin where there'd been a storage area and gasped when I saw what Logan had created.

It was freaking beautiful.

My new bathroom was small but elegant, with a simple, white pedestal vanity with gold-toned fixtures, matching toilet, and a gleaming tiled shower.

"What do you think?" Logan asked, moving aside so I could enter.

I carefully stepped over nails and other construction scrap, and ran my fingers along the smooth new drywall waiting for paint.

"Oh my god, Logan. It's perfection," I said breathlessly, spinning around to take it all in.

I ran to him and threw my arms around his neck. "Oh, thank you, thank you, thank you. It's beautiful."

When I let him go, I opened the glass shower door to admire his tile work. "I can't believe how fast you got this done."

Logan nodded. "Yeah, well when building houses is your business, you get pretty fast. Plus, Theo and Colton pitched in."

I looked around. "Where are they?"

He pointed. "They're out back, laying the water pipe."

I ran to thank them, too.

"Hey, beautiful," Colton said, wiping sweat from his brow. "You like what you see?"

I threw my hands up in the air. How would I even begin to thank them? "It's amazing. So amazing. I'm thrilled."

The funny thing was, the bathroom was so nice that now the rest of the cabin was more dowdy than ever.

But I was not complaining. Not at all.

"Ava, I think it's high time we dismantle that nasty old outhouse."

I'd never heard more beautiful words. "Oh my god, yes."

He handed me a huge, heavy pickaxe. In fact, I could barely lift it.

"Why don't you take the first swipe at the thing? Then, my brother and I will finish it."

I laughed gleefully. This was better than being a kid on Christmas morning.

"Here. Let's hold it together. I'll help you swing."

I jumped up and down.

Theo got behind me, and together, we held the axe as if he were teaching me how to swing a baseball bat. We wound up and swung hard, right into the outhouse door, which split apart with a booming crack.

I squealed at the power of the heavy tool. Who knew destroying things could be so much fun?

Theo laughed. "Good job. One hit and the whole door is practically gone. Maybe I should let you finish the whole thing."

"I could be talked into that." I pulled open what was left of the door, dangling from its hinges, to see inside the nasty place one last time before it became a pile of firewood.

Interesting.

The strike against the door had also split open the outhouse floor.

And exposed something shiny.

"What is that?" Theo said, Colton peering over his shoulder.

I crouched to get a better look. "Yeah. What the heck is it?" I reached for it, but it was stuck under something.

"Here. Step back," Theo said. He heaved the pickaxe up and brought it down on the outhouse floor, splitting the rotten wood wide open, revealing an old metal lock box.

He pulled it out of the debris and handed it to me.

I turned the cold, weighty metal over in my hands. It looked familiar. It felt familiar, too.

And then it occurred to me. My mother had one just like it. Her father had given it to her when she got married.

Maybe Gramps had given Uncle Bo his, too?

When I shook it, I heard the quiet sound of something dull rolling around inside. I knelt to the ground and set it before me with Colton and Theo watching, their faces puzzled.

I heard Logan coming up behind me and turned to show him the box. "What's that?"

I ran my hand over the smooth metal, spattered with chunky dust and dirt. "We just found under the floor in the outhouse."

Logan crouched for a closer look. "No kidding. That thing was in the *outhouse?*"

I nodded, still dumbstruck by our finding.

"Is it locked?" Theo asked.

I pressed the latch in a couple directions until I heard a small spring give way, and the top opened a quarter inch.

What was a metal box doing in Uncle Bo's freaking outhouse?"

I hoped he wasn't into anything illegal.

I cautiously lifted the lid, reaching into it and rustling through its contents.

"What is it, Ava? C'mon," Theo chided.

"No freaking way," I breathed.

Theo leaned over and looked in the box himself. "Well, would you look at that?"

"What? What the hell is it?" Logan asked.

I scooped part of the contents into my hands and held it out for everyone to see.

It took me a moment to find my voice.

When I finally did, I dropped the box onto the ground, and scooped out even more.

"It's money. Lots of money. Like *hundred-dollar bills,* money."

COLTON PAYNE

"So, the old bastard was loaded all this time. No wonder he could court all those hot babes and spend the winter in Key West doing body painting. And whatever else he did down there."

Ava, holding stacks of money like she couldn't believe her eyes, shot me the stink eye. I think she was happy to get to know her uncle through our crazy stories, but there was a limit to the amount of detail she wanted.

Guess I wouldn't tell her I'd heard through the grapevine Bo had actually died having a threesome with two twenty-year old lovelies.

Yeah, Ava didn't need to know that.

She pulled an envelope out of the bottom of the lock box and held it up.

"He left me a note." She stared at it in her hands turning it over like she was afraid to open it.

Theo glanced my way. "Do you want some privacy? You know, while you read it?"

Fuck that, I wanted to know what it said.

She shook her head anyway. "No. Thank you. There's nothing to hide, especially since you all knew him better than I did."

After looking at it for a moment longer, she tore it open, pulling out what looked like, at least from where I stood, a brief letter scrawled in old-man handwriting.

She read it out loud:

Dear Ava:

If you're reading this, that means I'm most likely gone and that you are tearing down the outhouse, which also means you are probably fixing up the cabin. Just think, if you'd sold the place without getting rid of the outhouse, someone else further down the line would have found this money. If you are that someone, you've just won the jackpot. Good for you.

Sorry to leave the place in such a mess, but I know you are a capable girl and will figure out the right thing to do. This money will help with whatever direction you decide to go in. Put it toward the cabin, and use the rest for whatever.

One last thing. If you haven't already met them, I have some great neighbors: Logan, Theo, and Colton. They're good men. And, at this writing, they are single.

Your loving uncle, Bo

Holy shit. "He called us out in his letter," I said, taking the note to read for myself.

I didn't know why, but his remembering us made me feel pretty damn good.

Ava sat there in the ground, in a daze, bouncing the rolls of hundreds around in her hands.

"How much do you think it is?" Logan asked.

Ava took a deep breath and fanned the end of the one of the stacks, held together with a thick rubber band. "I... I don't know."

Logan picked up a stack and tossed it up and down to assess its weight. "If these bills are all hundreds, which they appear to be, I'd say there's about a hundred in each bundle. How many bundles are there?" he asked, gesturing toward the box.

Ava counted them up quickly. "Ten including the one in your hand. Ten altogether."

Logan's eyes widened. "In that case, I'd say you have around a hundred thousand dollars."

Ava's mouth dropped open.

That son of a bitch had stashed money away for his niece. Incredible.

"Ava's buying lunch." Theo laughed.

Pale and frowning, she didn't look all that excited. She got to her feet and turned to Logan. "I can pay you. Here, take some of this."

He frowned and held his hand up. "No. I told you, Ava, I'm not taking payment for my work."

She looked into the woods, a confused expression overtaking her pretty face. "I... I don't need the money from the cabin anymore. I have this."

She stared at the contents of the lock box. "I have to go home. Right now."

Theo put his hands up. "Why? Why do you have to leave now?"

"I have to take care of some things. I... I'll be back, though."

Mumbling, she ran into the house and not five minutes later was heading down the driveway in her VW Bug.

Before she left, she'd kissed us all goodbye. "I'll be back in touch. I have to take care of something."

Logan, Theo, and I sat on the cabin front steps, dumb-founded by what had just happened. We didn't know which was stranger, that Ava found that money, or that she took off like her ass was on fire.

"Do you think she's coming back?" Theo asked.

Logan shook his head. "Doubt it. I mean, she was up here to cash out. She doesn't need the proceeds from the cabin anymore. I'll bet she calls the real estate agent and tells him to dump the place."

It kind of made me pissed that Logan had put all that time into the repairs, not to mention built the bathroom.

"Shit. She's gone," he said, slapping his thighs and heading back into the house.

"Where are you going?" I asked.

He shrugged with one shoulder. "I'm gonna finish what I started, then get the hell out of here." He disap-peared into the house.

Logan didn't give much away, but I knew him well enough to know he was not happy.

My brother and I looked at each other. "She'll be back," Theo said. "She had a real connection with all of us.

I patted him on the back. "I don't know, Bro. I hope she does return. But if not, I wouldn't be surprised."

I would, however, be bummed. Ava was the first woman I'd felt anything for since the debacle with my former fiancé. She'd shown me I could love again.

There. I'd said it.

And fuck it if anyone didn't like it.

She had to come back to Deep Water. She had to.

I left Logan working on the bathroom and Theo staring into the distance. I made my way back over the bridge and to our own house to be alone and process what the fuck had just happened.

Only the evening before, we'd had a freaking awesome sexy session with Ava. I knew I had feelings for her, and I thought she did for me, too. Had I read her that wrong?

And were the others thinking the same at that moment?

More importantly, while Ava might be driving like a bat out of hell down the mountain, what was *she* thinking?

32

AVA STONE

"So, you're really doing it?"

My boss looked at me suspiciously.

I loved how she did that, challenged me. I was going to miss the hell out of her.

I looked around her office, where I'd spent so much time, first as an intern, then as her assistant, and after that as one of the agency's account executives. This woman had believed in me and given me every professional opportunity I'd ever had.

She'd also kicked my ass mercilessly, but I didn't hold that against her.

I shrugged, still amazed with how my life had changed in what was really just a few days. "I am. I can't believe it myself. You'll come visit me, won't you?"

She hesitated for a sec, then examined her manicure.

I had done the same not long before, myself.

Some things were hard to give up. Others, not so much.

"I don't really do mountains…" she started to say.

Sounded familiar… but I tuned her out, if only for a moment. I knew where she was coming from, and I couldn't judge.

After I'd found Bo's money, something had come over me. I'd had to get off the mountain immediately. I didn't expect to be gone for long, but I just needed to clear my head and more importantly, find out if, when I was back in the city, I still longed for the same things I had the day I'd left.

And I didn't. Which was not only a relief but also made me very happy.

I told my mother about the money.

"Oh, honey, I'm glad he left that to you. That's probably the money he got when your grandfather died thirty years ago. I got the same. Used it for the house your father and I live in right now."

"You never said anything about that before," I said.

"Hmmm. Guess not. I just never thought it was important, how we bought the house. What I do think is interesting, though, is how Bo didn't use his to buy his own house. Or fix up the cabin."

"Guess he really liked it the way it was," I said.

"Obviously. Each to their own."

I continued stuffing things in large green garbage bags. I could have used suitcases, but this was faster and besides, where I was going, these sorts of things didn't matter. And the bags would be re-usable.

"Mom, why do you think he left everything to me?"

She was quiet for a moment. "I think that, even when you were a kid, he saw something of himself in you."

I'd been like *him*? Then how the hell did I get so off track, with my corporate goals and materialistic desires?

My voice caught. "I feel so badly now that we didn't keep up with him all these years. I wonder if he was lonely."

"Oh, I don't know about that, honey. He always had a lot of friends."

Lady friends for sure. But I didn't go there with Mom.

"You know," she continued, "it wasn't his doing. I cut him out. I was not a good sister. I've known that for a long time. I just didn't know how to mend the rift and now it's too late."

And now, Mom's voice caught.

She cleared her throat. She was not a crier and would do anything to avoid shedding a tear. Unlike me.

"I have to say, Ava, I'm concerned that you'll be isolated up there at the cabin. Promise me you'll come back down frequently and visit."

"Of course I will, Mom."

Hmmm. Was this a good time to tell her about the guys?

But what the hell would I say? That I was doing three mountain men who all lived together and had been friends of Bo's? And who were the most gorgeous men I'd ever known?

And who knew if they really wanted me, anyway. They'd talked about sharing, but I still wasn't sure what the hell that meant.

"What about work?" she asked.

"My boss wouldn't let me completely resign, which is probably a good thing. She told me to just take a leave of absence in case I wanted to come back. I think she just wants to be able to call me if she gets in a jam."

"How will you get by?" she asked.

"Bo's money will last me for a while. Plus, I have some ideas."

She laughed. "Ava, you've never had any shortage of ideas."

Maybe that was what Bo liked about me?

THERE I WAS TRUCKING up the mountain again, this time with my car packed to the gills. In fact, I had so much shit stuffed into my car that the poor VW was actually slower than usual climbing hills, which wasn't saying much. Thank god there wasn't any traffic, because I'd surely be holding it up.

What a difference a couple weeks made. This time, I was heading up to the mountain with a full tank of gas. I wasn't going to make that mistake again, although if Logan pulled over to help me, I was pretty sure I knew what kind of fun we'd have.

And this time, I wasn't wearing the high-heeled

designer boots that I'd put on my credit card last year and had taken months to pay off.

Why had I done stupid shit like that?

Oh right, I did it because I thought I was supposed to.

Although, I had to admit, I did have the fancy boots with me. I hadn't spent all that damn money for nothing. But I had a feeling they were going to be dust collectors more than anything else.

For the drive up the mountain, I'd simply worn my sneakers.

Yup, I was becoming a sneakers and jeans kind of girl.

The guys would be pleased to see I'd bought myself some proper hiking boots. Not that I planned to hike. But just in case I changed my mind.

Speaking of the guys, I wasn't at all sure they'd have me, especially with the way I'd taken off when I'd found Bo's money. They probably thought I was a damn flake to just leave the cabin mid-construction.

And to leave them with no explanation.

I could have called them while I was gone. But I had some thinking to do.

And I could have called them while I was on my way back up. But the conversation I planned to have needed to be in person.

I FINALLY ARRIVED at the cabin late that night in the pitch dark. But I knew enough to keep my headlights on the house until I got to the door and could switch on the house lights.

And as the front of the house was illuminated by my car, I saw something was off.

Something was different.

I couldn't see well in the dark, but there was enough light to see that a new porch railing had been built, and as I got closer, that a porch swing had been hung on the far end.

A *porch swing*?

Who the hell had done that?

Actually, I knew the answer.

Using my key, I was happy to see the front door lock worked. Not that I expected any less of Logan's work, I'd just been traumatized that my first experience with the cabin was that the damn door had no lock.

But it was when I flipped on the inside light that I really almost had a heart attack.

Holy fucking shit.

The rough, exposed wood of Bo's cabin was gone. In its place was the same exact wood, but it had been sanded, the holes filled in, and varnished a beautiful brown-gold.

The floors were re-finished, and covered with a couple plushy throw rugs.

The area where the kitchen table had been was now home to a new dining table surrounded by six rustic leather chairs. I pulled one out to take a seat before I fainted. The wood of the table was thick and heavy but had been smoothed out on the top and sides.

Spotting a shadow on the table, I looked up and saw

that the naked lightbulb that had previously struggled to illuminate the cabin had been replaced by not one but two chandeliers made of antlers.

What the hell had happened while I'd been gone?

I ran to the bedrooms. One of them had been outfitted with two brass twin beds with matching quilts and pillows. The other had a lovely wooden bed frame under Bo's expensive designer mattress. The walls had been stained an antique-y silver-gray, and a nightstand had been added, which someone had piled a few of Bo's books on top of.

I'd forgotten to check out the kitchen.

Wowsa.

Bo's nasty cabinets had been painted a glossy white, lightening up the formerly dark, dreary room.

I walked around, marveling at the complete transformation of Uncle Bo's cabin. Of course, I knew who was behind it. I knew better than to think some stranger had come in here and done all this. I wanted to not only thank the guys but also scold them for putting so much back-breaking work into my cabin when I certainly didn't deserve their efforts.

I ran my hand over the new sectional sofa in the living room, which made for a nice amount of seating as well as a place to take an afternoon nap. I flicked on the TV using the remote and found an old episode of *Friends* after clicking through Netflix, HBO, and a bunch of other streaming services.

Wait. Someone had added internet to the cabin.

How perfect.

I woke up early the next morning, stiff from having fallen asleep sitting up and with all my clothes on. I must have turned off the TV at some point, because it wasn't even warm to the touch.

And then it occurred to me.

Shit.

I ran outside to the car where I'd left the headlights on when I was entering the house. I'd never turned them off.

Stupid.

And now I had a dead battery, because of course. But I still grabbed a bunch of my crap and lugged it into the house.

All the more reason to call on my hunky neighbors.

I dropped my garbage bags in the middle of the floor, marveling over the cabin's transformation, which was more impressive in the daylight, if that were possible. I could now see the painstaking care that had been put into all the renovations, and I felt like even more of an idiot for bailing the way I had.

Why had they done this for me?

Had they known I'd be coming back?

I plopped down on my bed with my head in my hands. Had I fucked up? Was there still a chance for all of us?

Or were they just trying to fix up the cabin so it would easily sell and they could get new neighbors?

I made myself toast and screwed up all my courage. It was time to head over the bridge and see if I'd completely fucked up my life.

33

LOGAN MEYER

WHO THE HELL HAD JUST KNOCKED ON OUR DOOR?

Nobody ever knocked on our door. If they knew us well enough to show up, they knew us well enough to just freaking walk in.

And given that we were off the beaten path, we didn't exactly get kids selling candy bars for their school fundraisers.

If it was one of the guys pranking me, I was going to be seriously irritated. It was too early in the morning for that shit.

As I passed out of my bedroom, I heard snoring coming from Theo's room, and Colton's door was open just enough to see he was still snoozing, too.

I padded across the house in my boxers, not really caring if they were decent or not. Knocking on our door at that hour was borderline indecent, if you asked me. And whoever was paying us a visit was going to hear my opinion on the matter.

Strangely, by the time I got to the door, the knocking had stopped.

I returned to my room. Dodged that bullet.

But then it started again.

"Oh, for Christ's sake," I mumbled, storming back to the front of the house.

I reluctantly yanked the door open to see what was waiting on the other side.

What?

"Why didn't you tell us you were coming?"

Ava's bottom lip trembled, and next I knew, she'd thrown herself into my arms.

"Oh my god, Logan, thank you for all you've done," she sobbed into my shoulder.

I thought she might like all the work we had done on the house. We'd even recruited some other friends to help so we could get the work done extra-fast. They were all old friends of Bo's, too, so it had been a roaring good time, especially as we finished off all his cheap booze.

"Well, look who it is," Colton said from behind me.

Ava looked up and ran to him, almost knocking him over with her momentum.

"Easy girl, easy," he laughed, spinning her off her feet. "Hey, why the tears?" he asked, pulling back to take a look at her.

She sniffled. "You guys… you guys did not have to… do all that work on the cabin. You shouldn't have done it. I don't deserve it." She wiped her eyes with the back of her hand.

All the commotion must have awoken Theo, whose snoring normally drowned out any ambient noise.

"Holy shit, it's Ava!" Theo hollered, scooping her up and twirling her like his brother had. "You're back. I knew you'd be back." He planted a big, juicy kiss right on her lips.

It was true. Theo, ever the optimist, had said all along that Ava would be back. That she just needed time to straighten her head out.

I hadn't been so sure, but not to pat myself, or anyone, on our backs, but we had a pretty good thing going with her.

At least we all thought so.

But the longer she stayed away with zero communication, the more I became convinced we'd seen the last of her.

I'd never been so happy to be wrong.

"I'm back," she croaked.

"I can see that." I laughed. "What happened?"

Colton took her by the hand and let her to the sofa. "Yeah. Fill us in."

She took a deep breath. "I freaked when I saw all that money from Bo. I don't know what came over me, but I suddenly felt like I couldn't breathe. I had to get out of the cabin. It was like I was too close to it to make any decisions about what I should do."

She looked down at her hands. "And too close to make a decision about all of you."

Ah. What I'd been waiting for.

Just because she was back up on the mountain did not mean she was either here permanently, or had decided to see how things went with us. I wasn't taking anything for granted. It was part of having been part of the business world.

Theo, on the other hand, who'd led a slightly more sheltered life, looked thrilled. I had no doubt he'd jumped to all sorts of conclusions about what Ava's future on the mountain with us looked like.

Cynicism was just not part of his DNA.

And now that our lovely girl was before us, regardless of how long she was or was not staying, I found myself thinking of kissing her.

And more.

But that would have to wait, if it were to happen at all.

It's funny how life teaches you a lesson when you least expect it. For years, I'd wanted my dad to get off my back with his accusations about ruining his business, and therefore his life. I'd been wracked with guilt over his words and how it had broken our once-happy family in two.

But I'd finally accepted that there was no way I was responsible for the old man's happiness. If he didn't have his failed business to bitch at me about, he would have just found something else.

The saddest part wasn't what I had missed out on. It

was the years of happiness my mother had been entitled to, which never came her way. That's what broke my heart.

I'd recently spoken to her about coming up to the mountain for a while if she were well enough. She'd be comfortable in the spare bedroom.

I just had to get Colton to stop walking around naked.

And now that I wasn't looking to my dad for approval of any sort, I felt like I could breathe.

Had Ava's coming on the scene had anything to do with my realization?

Who knew? There were many reasons to be happy, including finding a good woman to love.

But I was getting ahead of myself.

"So, what are you thinking, baby?" Colton asked.

He had balls. I was actually too fucking chicken to ask. Too afraid of getting bad news.

But Colton was tough. He'd been in the Army and lived a lifetime in the few years he was in the Middle East. He'd seen some crazy shit.

She took a deep breath, and for a moment, my heart stopped. "If… if you will have me, I'm on board."

I jumped up and swept her off her feet. I couldn't help it. This was what I'd wanted so badly I'd not dared let myself imagine it happening.

"Are you moving in with us, baby?" I asked in between the kisses I was raining down on her.

"I do want to enjoy Bo's cabin, and all the work you put into it. But I am staying. If you'll have me."

Theo and Colton high-fived each other.

"You see," she continued, "I'd been looking for one good reason to stick around Deep Water Mountain. And I finally realized I had three."

EPILOGUE

I have so many questions I wish I could ask my Uncle Bo, a man who lived large but who was also surrounded by a certain amount of mystery.

For example, I went through a box of his things squirreled away in the back of his clothes closet, behind another pile of Playboys. In it, I found pictures of a child, ranging from baby to toddler age.

Did he have a kid with some woman? And if so, why did the photos stop coming?

Was there someone walking the face of the earth who didn't know that Bo was their dad? If so, they were missing out on the story of a fascinating man.

But things like that are complicated, so maybe the way things turned out was for the best.

I know the way things turned out for me have been for the best.

After some back and forth, and struggling to say goodbye to my old 'city life,' not to mention manicures, designer boots, and cashmere sweaters, I'd finally landed on Deep Water Mountain permanently. Well, as permanently as anything in life.

I planned to go back to the city every few months, and I didn't have to worry about being lonely because my girlfriends had been rotating their visits. Who knew so many of my friends would take advantage of a cabin in the mountains where they could stay for free anytime they wanted?

My boss had come to visit, too, and even brought hiking boots. Now that about knocked me off my chair.

Mom had been to visit once she found out I'd had a bathroom installed. We scattered Bo's ashes in the creek, and she actually shed a few tears. I think she felt good that my keeping the cabin gave her a connection to her older, estranged brother. Like she was sort of getting another chance to connect with him. She even walked down to the pond by herself. I found her sitting in the same spot where I'd had sex with Colton not long before. 'Course, I didn't tell her that.

While I was able to keep earning a small living from doing odd bits of work for the PR firm thanks to my ultra-cool boss, my main project was writing a new book, which I was sure was going to be a big hit. No one was surprised by the title: The City Girl's Guide to Making it in the Mountains. *Kind of long, but it has a good ring to it.*

The research for it has been crazy. Like, I found out what the early pioneering women used when they had their periods.

Yeah, that part I won't be putting in the book.

The best part of my new life was, of course, the guys.

Logan, my smooth-headed home builder, was putting together a new outbuilding on Bo's property where the outhouse had once been. It's sort of a combination guest house-slash-office for me to work on my book in.

Not surprisingly, he made sure there was a comfortable little bed in it. You know, for taking breaks and stuff.

He was super busy now and I don't think spent any time at all ruminating over his father any more.

My favorite hippie dude, Theo, had talked all of us into trying his meditation retreat and he was thrilled beyond words that he might have some converts. Actually, I think the other guys caved when I'd been so enthusiastic about it. It was to be a two-night camping trip, where we'd each stay in one huge tent, all together. I wasn't sure how much meditation was going to happen, but I was certain it would be a lot of fun. And steamy.

I'd taken him to the city on one or two trips, and while he'd loved it, I could tell he was always relieved to get back to Deep Water. I felt the same way.

Colton, my quiet military man, continued to hunt and fish and cook us delicious meals. Theo said he hadn't seen his brother so happy since before he'd left for the Middle East. I don't know if I agreed, but he seemed to think I had something to do with it.

I wish my uncle could know how many people he'd made happy with his decision to leave me his cabin. Even if it were a fixer-upper.

It's almost like he knew how much the guys liked a fixer-upper. And that I would be their most successful project, ever.

Did you like *Her Dirty Mountain Men?*
Learn about the next book in the Men at Work series,
Her Dirty Soldiers.

I hope you loved reading this book as much as I loved writing it. Please visit my store to learn more about my books, and to buy directly from me!
https://mikalaneshop.com/

Dear Reader:

I'm USA TODAY bestselling romance author Mika Lane, and am OBSESSED with bringing you sassy, steamy stories with imperfect heroines and the bad-a*s dudes they bring to their knees. I'll always bring you my signature humor and heat, topped off with a modern-day happily ever after.

My first book ever was *The Day I Ate the Milkyway,* a true fourth-grade masterpiece illustrated with crayons and bound with construction paper and glue. Nowadays, steamy romance gives purpose to my days and nights as I create worlds and characters that tickle the imagination. I live in magical Northern California with my own handsome alpha dude, sometimes known as Mr. Mika Lane, and two devilish cats named Chuck and Murray.

A dual citizen of the United States and Ireland, I have on more than one occasion spent my last dollar on a plane ticket somewhere, and am always planning my next escape. I often try new recipes on unsuspecting friends, search out hiding places to read undisturbed, and sadly kill every houseplant I bring home.

I LOVE to hear from readers when I'm not dreaming up naughty tales to share. Visit my online shop https://mikalaneshop.com/ and say hello https://mikalaneshop.com/pages/meet-mika.

xoxo, Mika

www.ingramcontent.com/pod-product-compliance
Lightning Source LLC
Chambersburg PA
CBHW011151190726
48288CB00010B/3276